Best wishes,

Alan Bleasdale

Liverpool 1986

NO SURRENDER

By the same author

'ARE YOU LONESOME TONIGHT?'

NO SURRENDER
A Deadpan Farce

ALAN BLEASDALE

ff

faber and faber

LONDON · BOSTON

First published in 1986
by Faber and Faber Limited
3 Queen Square London WC1N 3AU

Filmset by Wilmaset, Birkenhead, Wirral
Printed in Great Britain by
Redwood Burn Ltd, Trowbridge, Wiltshire
All rights reserved

British Library Cataloguing in Publication Data

Bleasdale, Alan
No surrender.
I. Title
791.43'72   PN1997

ISBN 0-571-13769-5

Library of Congress Cataloging-in-Publication Data

Bleasdale, Alan.
No surrender.
I. Title
PN1997.N524B5   1986   791.43'72   85-20457
ISBN 0-571-13769-5 (pbk.)

No Surrender opened in London in early 1986. The cast included the following:

MIKE	Michael Angelis
MARTHA O'GORMAN	Avis Bunnage
PADDY BURKE	James Ellis
MR ROSS	Tom Georgeson
BERNARD	Bernard Hill
BILLY MCRACKEN	Ray McAnally
NORMAN	Mark Mulholland
CHERYL	Joanne Whalley
GEORGE O'GORMAN	J. G. Devlin
FRANK	Vince Earl
RONNY	Ken Jones
TONY BONAPARTE	Michael Ripper
BARBARA	Marjorie Sudell
SUPERWOMAN	Joan Turner

Executive Producer	Michael Peacock
Producer	Mamoun Hassan
Director	Peter Smith
Music	Daryl Runswick
Production Designer	Andrew Mollo
Director of Photography	Mick Coulter
Editor	Rodney Holland
Supervising Editor	Kevin Brownlow

A Dumbarton Films Production in association with National Film Finance Corporation/Film Four International and William Johnston/Ronald Lillie/Lauron International Inc.

EXT. WALLASEY PROMENADE. FACING THE RIVER MERSEY.
DUSK.
*One of several four-sided shelters – the side facing the promenade
and the river.*
An old man, an ULSTERMAN, *guttural and gutterlike, sits alone. In
a corner, huddled up. Cornered. Freezing. A large bottle of Irish
whiskey in his mittened hands is two-thirds empty.*
The sound of people approaching. A dog barks. The ULSTERMAN
*twitches to life. Puts his whiskey away. Hesitates. Goes to peep
around the shelter. Stops. Huddles up even more. Waits.*
*A middle-aged couple briskly walking their dog. They stride past.
Unseeing.*
The ULSTERMAN *waits till they are out of earshot.*
ULSTERMAN: . . . Come on, *come on.* (*He shuffles back into his
    coat pockets for the whiskey.*)

EXT. WALLASEY PROMENADE. DUSK.
The shelter facing the river.
The ULSTERMAN *waits. The noise of a car approaching. Slowly.
The* ULSTERMAN *fidgets nervously towards the edge of the shelter.
The car is coming nearer. Then stops. The* ULSTERMAN *doesn't
know whether to look or not.*
*Sound of the car door being opened, then closed. Footsteps approaching.
The hint of someone heavy-footed and slow. Finally we see a brick
outhouse of a man. Staring into the shelter towards the* ULSTERMAN.
ULSTERMAN: Billy! . . . It is you, isn't it, Billy?
BILLY: It's me.
    (*The* ULSTERMAN *comes to life. Exuberantly. Jumps up and
    dances forward, slaps and hugs* BILLY.)
ULSTERMAN: Billy! Billy Boy!
    (*The* ULSTERMAN *stands and shadow boxes in front of the
    much bigger man. We see* BILLY *properly as the scene develops.
    He has been a big fit boyo and buck once. Now gone to seed
    and alcohol. And hardening of the arteries. He has an Ulster
    accent that has been practising Liverpool for forty-five years.*)

9

Hey! Hey! Hoy-hoh! Me and you, Billy! Me and you! Billy
the Beast and me!

BILLY: What is it you want? There are things I have to do. I
have obligations tonight.

ULSTERMAN: And here's me all the way over from Belfast just
to see you special. You and me were friends, Billy. We
fought together. That's an obligation in itself, surely?

BILLY: Is it?

ULSTERMAN: Of course it is, and I have kept in touch. In me
own fashion.

BILLY: Not so that I've noticed.

ULSTERMAN: Oh but I have, Billy, I have . . . You'd be
surprised.

BILLY: Nothing surprises me these days, Norman. Not even
this.

ULSTERMAN: Sit down and have a drink, Billy. For old times'
sake and the new year coming.

BILLY: Nah, you don't get a good pint in there. Noted for it.

ULSTERMAN: Away to that and behave yourself, you would have
drunk battery acid once.

BILLY: I would have done a lot of things once. I'll stay as I am.
I've told you, I'm in a hurry. Speak your mind and then I'll

go. Speak your weight if you want, I don't much care. (*The* ULSTERMAN *sits down.*)

ULSTERMAN: . . . I'm on the run.

(BILLY *laughs.*)

What is so funny about that?

BILLY: On the run, you won't get far. Not at your age.

ULSTERMAN: *This is serious.*

BILLY: I doubt it, seriously.

ULSTERMAN: It's for a good cause, Billy. For God and Ulster. (*No reply.* BILLY *looks at his watch.*)

There are some who are still following in your footsteps.

BILLY: They'll be walkin' in a good deal of shite then. I have to go now. (BILLY *walks away.*)

ULSTERMAN: No surrender, Billy. *No fucking Surrender!* (BILLY *stands by his car. Puts his hands in the air.*)

BILLY: I surrender. In fact, I give up.

ULSTERMAN: 'Course, I understand why, we all do.

BILLY: . . . Oh aye?

ULSTERMAN: I mean, it was an awful shame about your daughter. . . . You know the daughter I mean?

BILLY: I have three daughters.

ULSTERMAN: But only one of them went back to Northern Ireland and made a fool of herself. And you. A whirlwind romance. A sudden marriage. To a Catholic, Billy. A strong Catholic. A loud Catholic. One troublesome Catholic.

BILLY: I know, I know, but she is happy.

ULSTERMAN: Well, a whole lot of other people are not.

BILLY: (*Angry*) Look, Norman, my father died a pauper in this city, starved from our own land, to come and starve here. He had nothing to give me, my da', but he left me three things when he died – my religion, my politics and my football team – all true blue. *It's still the same*, I still have it all, I will never talk to the Catholic boy . . . I won't have anything to do with him. (*He has almost run out of breath and energy.*) . . . but the violence of it all has left me. I'm a member of the Orange Order and proud of it. But I am not a mad young gunman any more.

ULSTERMAN: We have her address, Billy. I can even remember the road without reference to my . . . files.

(*A long pause.* BILLY *leans against the car.*)
I have looked after her, Billy. I have made sure she did not
become a widow. For old times' sake. For the days when
we both were 'mad' and we both carried guns and went to
prison. I told you I had still kept in touch.
(*Another long pause.*)
BILLY: I don't believe you.
ULSTERMAN: Number fourteen. Ladyfields Road,
    Ballymurphy.
BILLY: What do you want?
    (*The* ULSTERMAN *motions* BILLY *back towards the shelter.*)
ULSTERMAN: Come and have a wee drink, Billy. Come on . . .
    (BILLY *slowly sags towards the shelter with the* ULSTERMAN.)

EXT. TERRACED STREET IN TOXTETH, LEADING DOWN TO
RIVER. DAY.
MIKE, *a bearded man in his late thirties, carrying a suit bag. Leaves his
house and approaches a kind of car best described as 'rust-coloured'.*

EXT. MIKE DRIVING THROUGH THE INNER-CITY STREETS OF
LIVERPOOL. DAY.
*The dismal destroyed tenement slums and, appropriately, a Job
Centre, boarded up and closed down.*

EXT. THE CHARLESTON CLUB. DUSK.
*It has never seen better days. Liverpool's answer to Blackpool's reply
to Las Vegas. And the inside is worse.*
The rust-coloured hatchback car comes to a halt in the car park.
MIKE *gets out of the car. He pulls his dress suit, on a hanger in his
suit bag, out of the back of the car. Looks around. Flatly.*
*Four kids approach the car. On push-bikes. One is smoking. He is
the oldest. He is twelve.*
KID: Look after your car, mister?
MIKE: What for?
SMOKING KID: 'Cos otherwise it won't fucking well be here
    when you get back.
MIKE: I can see you've had a pleasant Christmas, deep in the
    bosom of your family.
SMOKING KID: Y' wha?

MIKE: How much?

SMOKING KID: A quid.

> (MIKE *reluctantly dips into his pocket.*)
>
> (*Grinning affably*) Each.

MIKE: On y' bike. Here. Happy New Year. Have an accident.

> (*He flicks the money at them, and turns away. The* SMOKING KID *follows him.*)

SMOKING KID: Got any ciggies?

MIKE: I don't smoke.

SMOKING KID: Y' will do when y've come out of there. It's death in there. They all come out cryin'. All the acts.

MIKE: I'm not an act. Now go on, beat it. Kill a midget or somethin'.

> (*He walks on. The* SMOKING KID *stops. Flicks his ciggie butt at* MIKE's *back.*
>
> MIKE *approaches the locked steel doors at the front of the club. Glances at his watch. Knocks on the doors. No answer. Knocks again. Again no answer. The* SMOKING KID *shouts to him.*)

SMOKING KID: I know where y' can get in the back way.

MIKE: (*To himself*) I bet y'do.

SMOKING KID: . . . But it'll cost y'.

> (MIKE *turns away and begins to move towards the back of the Charleston Club.*)

EXT. A SHAMBLES OF AN ESTATE. INNER-CITY LIVERPOOL. DUSK.

Focus on entrance to an underground passageway beneath a busy main road.

INT. UNDERGROUND PASSAGEWAY.

The place is piss-stained, littered and scrawled upon.
In the middle of the passageway there is a fork, and another passageway goes off sharply to the right.
There are two lads at this point in the shadows of the passageway. Close up, we see that they are scruffy, menacing and loitering. One is more scruffy, menacing and loitering than the other. They now speak in screeching whispers.

REAL MENACE: . . . Can you hear something?

UNCERTAIN MENACE: Yeah, me bottle. It's just fuckin' broken.

REAL MENACE: No, listen.
(*We can hear nothing.*)
UNCERTAIN MENACE: (*Not listening*) I dunno though, Degsie, for fuck's sake, this is the fuckin' pits. I was going to a party.
REAL MENACE: An' what were y' goin' with?
UNCERTAIN MENACE: A clear fuckin' conscience.
REAL MENACE: They don't take that at the off licence.
UNCERTAIN MENACE: . . . New Year's Fuckin' Eve. . . . I've got CSE certificates, y'know.
REAL MENACE: Shut up, will you! There's someone comin'.
(*And there is.*)
UNCERTAIN MENACE: Yeah, I know, someone with a fuckin' straitjacket. I'm here, I'm here, come 'head.
(REAL MENACE *digs him hard in the ribs. The footsteps come nearer. They wait in the angle of the fork, ready to spring out. One of them does, anyway.* UNCERTAIN MENACE *is rapidly being reduced to certain terror.*
A figure appears at the fork. Walking straight on.
In a flurry of action and overcoats, the youth with REAL MENACE *grabs and hurtles the new arrival towards the passageway that forks off.* UNCERTAIN MENACE *'joins in' from a distance. The third party's old holdall bounces and drops to the floor as he is bounced against and off the wall again. The two lads crowd in on him as* REAL MENACE *talks. The figure in the semi-darkness wears heavy-duty glasses. He tries, successfully, to keep them on.*)
REAL MENACE: All right, all right, no one's goin' to get hurt –
(*A white stick drops from out of the folds of the figure's overcoat, and clatters echoing on to the floor.*)
UNCERTAIN MENACE: Oh fuck! He's blind.
(*He goes to pick the white stick up.* REAL MENACE *relaxes his grip slightly. Hesitates for a second. Then pursues.*)
REAL MENACE: Look, pop, just give us what y've got an' we'll go.
UNCERTAIN MENACE: Let's just fuckin' go, f'fucks sake!
(*He goes to give the man his stick.*)
REAL MENACE: I'm not kiddin', give us it, come on, give us it!
(UNCERTAIN MENACE *is now close to the blind man.* REAL

MENACE *shakes the blind man. His glasses begin to spill towards the end of his nose. The blind man,* PADDY BURKE, *takes his glasses off with one hand as he talks, staring out unblinking.*)

PADDY BURKE: All right, all right, I'll give it to y'.

(*He takes the stick off* UNCERTAIN MENACE. *Both lads relax a touch.*

PADDY BURKE *butts* UNCERTAIN MENACE *full and foul in the face.* UNCERTAIN MENACE *drops like a dead weight. That howls.*

As UNCERTAIN MENACE *falls,* PADDY BURKE *turns on* REAL MENACE *who still has hold of him at an angle. He grabs the lad and hurls him against the opposite wall of the narrow passageway.* PADDY BURKE *follows after him quickly, listening for the noise of the collision with the wall, and begins to batter and slice at him with his white stick. Vicious cutting blows.*

No mercy.

Followed by the boot as the lad huddles to the ground. He too howls. Each time he howls, he gets hit again.)

UNCERTAIN MENACE: (*Through blood and a broken nose*) . . . Don't say anythin', Degsie – he can only hit y' if he can hear y'.

REAL MENACE: Oh fuck off, will y'. *Aaaggghhh!*

(*For some seconds more the lad takes the full brunt of the old man's violence in the shadows, before managing to crawl and cringe away.* UNCERTAIN MENACE, *holding his face with both hands, is already struggling off. They stumble away together. We faintly hear* REAL MENACE.)

. . . There was no fuckin' need for that . . .

(*We leave the scene as* PADDY BURKE *encounters the difficulty of trying to find his holdall on the floor. His stick beats out a rhythm of search till he finds it.*

He picks up his holdall, taps his stick against the wall till he finds the corner he wants. Puts his stick back inside his overcoat and continues his interrupted journey.)

EXT. THE SIDE OF THE CHARLESTON CLUB. DUSK.
MIKE *walks towards the back of the club. There is a gateway
leading to the tradesman's entrance. The gates are open.*
As MIKE *gets to within twenty yards of the gates, a gold-coloured
Mercedes screeches melodramatically around the corner leading to the
front of the club. The car races past him, five hunched shadows
barely seen in the car as it skids through the gateway and into the
'Courtyard' at the rear of the club.*
MIKE *hurries after the car. He turns into the courtyard in time to see
the back door of the club is open. And to see a man being hurtled into
the darkness through the doors. To land with a crash and a groan.
While three of the men in the car follow after him at a more leisurely
pace. The back door is slammed shut, as* MIKE *approaches. He
reaches the door. Hesitates. Considerably. Turns away.*
MIKE *sees the driver of the Mercedes watching him. The driver's eyes
follow him coldly. The automatic window on the driver's side begins
to slide down. The driver stares.*

16

MIKE: . . . What was all that about?

COLD EYES: Why? What's it to you?

MIKE: I just erm . . . I plan to . . . (*Points at the club*)
Nothing. It's just sort of not the normal way of entering a
night club.

COLD EYES: (*Flatly*) He forgot his coat. OK?
(*He winds up the window. In dismissal. MIKE hesitates. The
driver begins to put a chauffeur's cap on. Inspects the splendour
of it all in his driver's mirror. MIKE walks away.*)

EXT. NEAR HIGH RISE FLATS, LIVERPOOL. DUSK.

BILLY's *car. On a road driving through a housing estate. With the*
ULSTERMAN. *Silence. Finally:*

BILLY: . . . Y' a friggin' eejit, y'll spend y' dyin' days in
Dartmoor, prison . . .

ULSTERMAN: Not at all, I'll be all right. I'll lie low and slide
away when they've finished looking for me . . . we're nearly
there . . .
(*There are three big blocks of flats. Pensioners' flats, we will
discover. Amongst a group of maisonettes and houses.*)
Stop, here.
(*They stop. BILLY puts his head on the driving wheel.*)

BILLY: Well, that makes sense. A safe house in a block of
pensioners' flats.
(*The ULSTERMAN suddenly grabs BILLY's shoulder.*)

ULSTERMAN: Look! Billy, look!
(*He points to the gaps between the pensioners' flats. As one
police Transit quietly slides out of sight, another emerges, then
goes behind the building.*)
I've been blown, I've been blown.

BILLY: They pay good money to informers these days.

ULSTERMAN: Shut up, Billy, and just get out of here. Fast.
(*The car performs a tight, fast three-point turn.*)

BILLY: D'y' fancy a night out, Norman . . . ?

INT. PENSIONER'S FLAT, HIGH RISE.

*The bedroom. Dark brown makeup being liberally applied to a
white arm. Further away a big plastic false chest strapped to a big
benign-looking lady in her sixties. The plastic false chest has been*

coloured brown. The lady in full. BARBARA *in her grass skirt. Her hair is hennaed. Her body and face and limbs are brown. But not in the manner of the black-and-white minstrels. She is a West Indian limbo dancer.*

We hear a man's voice from outside. Her husband, RONNY.

RONNY: Hurry up, will y', love, it's gettin' late.

BARBARA: I'm doin' me best, Ronny. There's no point in doin' somethin' unless y' do y' best.

RONNY: What did y' make the tea for then?

(*He comes into the room. Grinning. Dressed as Davy Crockett and holding the Charleston Club invitation card.*)

BARBARA: What was wrong with the tea?

RONNY: Nothin', Barb, but come ahead though, girl.

BARBARA: Do you think I'll be all right, Ronny?

RONNY: Yeah, great as long as they set the limbo bar at five foot seven.

BARBARA: (*Indicating the card*) Tell me, y'know, about the fancy dress.

RONNY: (*Sighing not looking at the card*) First prize ten-day cruise for two, girl.

BARBARA: (*Coquettishly*) It's not to the West Indies by any chance, is it?

RONNY: (*Looks down*) Nah, Cardiff, Belfast, Glasgow and sunkissed Southern Iceland. (*Grins at her*) Dunno, doesn't say. (*Goes to turn away*) Still, ten days anywhere is better than being stuck here.

(*He goes out again, whistling 'Davy Crockett, King of the Wild Frontier . . .'*

He is about to go down the corridor leading from the front door, past the bedroom, and into the living-room, when we witness the front door being smashed off its hinges, and battered to the floor. Two large POLICEMEN *wearing flak jackets and carrying guns throw themselves into the corridor. At least four more follow them. In bedlam and screaming. From* RONNY *and* BARBARA *and the* POLICEMEN. RONNY *dashes back towards the bedroom door, and is knocked against the wall. His arms are thrust up in the air and he is searched. Some* POLICEMEN *race into the living room, and then race out again. Two have lurched into the bedroom.*)

BARBARA: Oh Christ, me angina!

(*The* POLICE, *the moment of madness gone, begin to be aware of the further madness. Six armed* POLICEMEN, *Davy Crockett and a West Indian limbo dancer.*)

RONNY: What the friggin' hell d' y' think y' doin'?

FIRST POLICEMAN: This is twenty-six?

RONNY: Yeah, an' this is someone with a heart complaint, I'll have you for this, you'll –

FIRST POLICEMAN: Is your name Norman Donohue?

RONNY: Is it shite.

(*He comforts a distraught* BARBARA *as best he can.*)

SECOND POLICEMAN: He is supposed to be Irish. I mean, he is Irish. He isn't.

FIRST POLICEMAN: But this is number twenty-six?

RONNY: Yeah, yeah, twenty-six Attlee Heights. Come 'head, girl . . .

(*The* POLICEMEN *look at each other and then away.*)

FIRST POLICEMAN: Attlee. This is Attlee. Not . . . Gaitskell?

RONNY: (*Not listening*) You've had it for this, you have.

(*Some of the* POLICEMEN *leave, talking in furious whispers on their walkie-talkies.*)

SECOND POLICEMAN: . . . We'll . . . on behalf, I'd . . . we'll get a carpenter straight out. Sir. We have them on standby. For incidents such as . . .

RONNY: I bet you do.

(*We leave them as* RONNY *comforts* BARBARA, *and one of the* POLICEMEN *contemplates what is left of the door.*)

EXT. THE FRONT OF THE CHARLESTON CLUB. DUSK.

MIKE *is banging on the door. Pause. No answer. He bangs again. Furiously. Constantly.*

Finally, a slit hole in the door opens. No more than four inches by three. A cruel mouth, a broken nose and heavily bagged eyes appear.

BROKEN NOSE: What's the score with you?

MIKE: I've been tryin' to get in f' half an hour.

BROKEN NOSE: We're not open. Not yet.

MIKE: Look, I'm going to be working here.

BROKEN NOSE: More fool you. (*Laughs.*)

MIKE: I am workin' here. Right now.

BROKEN NOSE: If y' an act, y' miles too early.

MIKE: No, I'm not an act, now open the door, will y'.

BROKEN NOSE: What are y' then?

MIKE: I'm the new manager. Is that good enough for y'?
    (BROKEN NOSE *stares at him. Up and down.*)

BROKEN NOSE: Not yet, no.
    (BROKEN NOSE *turns and shouts. Damaged eardrums time.*)
    Frank! . . .

MIKE: . . . I don't have to do this, y'know, I could be
    unemployed right now . . .

BROKEN NOSE: (*Louder still*) FRANK!

EXT. OUTSIDE A LOW LEVEL BLOCK OF FLATS. DUSK.

MR *and* MRS O'GORMAN. *Immaculate. Crippled. Deaf. She has
had a stroke, one side withered, and can barely walk at all. She
struggles along, her foot scraping, stick in hand, with stoic dignity.
He uses two sticks, in a strange rolling, balls-of-his-feet gait, almost
robot-like. It is as if he has to keep up his momentum up or he will
fall down. Consequently,* MR O'GORMAN *walks considerably faster.
He has to.*

*They are walking down the drive from the flats. He has, perhaps,
locked the doors, and is some yards behind her as we see them first.
We watch him overtake her, neither seeming to notice, as they
approach the minicab at the kerbside. The* CAB DRIVER *gets out and
opens the door for* MR O'GORMAN.

MINICAB DRIVER: Where to, Boss?

MR O'GORMAN: (*Loudly*) Do you know where we're going?

MINICAB DRIVER: No, I – (*Realizes. Shouts*) No, where do you
    want to go?

MR O'GORMAN: (*Loudly*) Twelfth of July Memorial Hall.

MINICAB DRIVER: Array, it's only down there. (*Points*)
    Can't you wa–

MR O'GORMAN: (*Loudly*) What?

MINICAB DRIVER: Nothin'. Nothin'. (*Shouts*) That's okay,
    Dad.

INT. MINICAB. DUSK.

MR O'GORMAN. MRS O'GORMAN. MINICAB DRIVER.

MRS O'GORMAN: What are we tonight?

MR O'GORMAN: What are we what?

MRS O'GORMAN: Are we Labour, Liberal, Conservative, Church of England, Roman Catholic, Help the Aged? Who's taking us out? I hate pretending to be Hebrew. I don't know any of their hymns.

MR O'GORMAN: (*For the benefit of the cab driver*) I've told you, woman, anyone'd think you were deaf!

MRS O'GORMAN: Pardon, George?

MR O'GORMAN: It's our own kind tonight. It's the Lodge, Martha. Billy's Boys. Penny Whistles and the Orange Sash!

MRS O'GORMAN: Oh hey, I hate them more than Help the Aged.

EXT. OUTSIDE THE TWELFTH OF JULY MEMORIAL HALL. DUSK.
The cab, containing MR *and* MRS O'GORMAN, *draws up outside hall.*

EXT. OUTSIDE THE CHARLESTON CLUB. DUSK.
MIKE *looks as though he has been there for some time.*
Sound of a door opening in the interior of the club. And then slamming definitely shut. BROKEN NOSE *opens the slit again. Looks at* MIKE. *He is moved aside by the approach of* FRANK. *Peering out. Looking, in close up, like* BROKEN NOSE's *younger brother. But with a brain. Of sorts.*

FRANK: . . . Yeah, that's him, I've seen his picture. Are you Greek or wha'?

MIKE: No, I've got a sunbed, now open the friggin' door.
(BROKEN NOSE *reluctantly opens the door.*)

EXT. THE TWELFTH OF JULY MEMORIAL HALL. DUSK.
MR O'GORMAN *follows* MRS O'GORMAN *into hall.*
As they go, and the MINICAB DRIVER *gets into his cab, we see* BILLY's *car come to a stop a few yards away.*
As the cab goes, we see the ULSTERMAN's *head slowly emerge from somewhere beneath the dashboard on the passenger's side.*

INT. THE TWELFTH OF JULY MEMORIAL HALL. DUSK.
*A small side room. Drab and bare apart from splashes of orange,
and the occasional framed pillowslip, embroidered by the Loyalist
internees, cage eleven, the Maze prison camp.*
The ULSTERMAN *slams a phone down, almost smashing it.* BILLY,
across the table, looks at him.
*The faint sound of 'Derry Walls' being played on accordion and
drums.*
BILLY: Nowhere left to go, Norman . . .
ULSTERMAN: But they should be there.
BILLY: Maybe they're on the run as well. Renewing old
    friendships. From forty years ago. That was the last time I
    saw you, Norman, forty years ago, in another city.
    (*The* ULSTERMAN *notices the contempt in* BILLY's *voice. For
    the first time, he seems tired and nervous.*)
ULSTERMAN: I had no one else to go to, Billy.
BILLY: So you came here to threaten my family.
ULSTERMAN: No, no, I came to you for help.
BILLY: You'd best come with me then.
ULSTERMAN: On a pissin' pensioners' outing?
BILLY: Well, you won't be out of place, will you?
    (BILLY *stands.*) And nobody else wants you. Norman.
    (*He moves to the door. Opens the door. We hear clearly, 'Derry
    Walls'.*)
    What's more you can sing all the old songs.
ULSTERMAN: I only want somewhere to go. Just for tonight
    even. I'll just try the boys one more time. (*Picks up the
    phone.*) Let them know where I'll be. . . . Where will I be?
BILLY: The Charleston Club, Stanley Road. Bring a pen as well,
    there's free bingo.
    (BILLY *closes the door. The* ULSTERMAN *dials furiously.
    Waits and waits.*)

INT. THE CHARLESTON CLUB. DUSK.
FRANK *and* BROKEN NOSE *in full. They are wider and taller than*
MIKE. *Both owe something to Brylcreem, and* BROKEN NOSE *has a
lapsed Teddy Boy's quiff. He is barely past forty but is already old
and broken and befuddled. A bouncer bounced once too often. He
has an open-necked dress shirt and a stained dinner jacket. The top*

button of his trousers is open, the zip slightly down. FRANK *wears clothes of the highest cost and lowest taste. Tom Jones's time.*
MIKE *will take in the glittering tattiness of the foyer as the scene develops. The destroyed carpets, the mismatched primal paintwork, peeling in places. The 'Stags and Hens' toilets, the almost cardboard cut-out cloakrooms, the handprinted announcements of forthcoming Attractions, the artistes' nicotine- and time-stained photographs. The space invaders and fruit machines. A cigarette machine. A pay phone. The signs: 'Sorry No Jeans'; 'Anyone who brings Spirits or Food into the Club will be asked to leave immediately, and refused re-entry'; 'The Management regrets that it cannot be held responsible for the nonappearance of Advertised Artistes . . . But it will do everything possible to secure adequate replacements'.*
Apathy.

BROKEN NOSE: Nobody's told me, not yet they haven't. I didn't know about no new manager.

MIKE: Y'know now.

BROKEN NOSE: But what's happened to McCarthur?

MIKE: He's going. We're doing this week together, then he's leaving.

FRANK: (*Shaking his head*) He's left.

MIKE: *What?*

FRANK: Only he's come back. Sort of like y'know when these famous rock bands split up. An' then they come back. If y' get me drift.

BROKEN NOSE: Er no, Frank. Not yet.

FRANK: He's givin' a final performance. An' he's goin' to sing.

BROKEN NOSE: Ah no, y' wrong there, he wouldn't do that, he's got a terrible voice.

MIKE: (*To* FRANK) You tryin' to tell me something?

BROKEN NOSE: No. I don't think so anyway.

FRANK: (*Putting his arm around* MIKE, *with all the warmth of a boa constrictor*) Don't worry, you'll find out. Soon enough. (*They are approaching the double doors leading into the body of the club. Another door is alongside. 'Private' and double locked.*)

MIKE: I'm really looking forward to it.

FRANK: I thought you might.

MIKE: But in the meantime, just as a matter of interest, merely to satisfy my curiosity, you haven't been a passenger in a Mercedes recently, have you?

FRANK: Could be, kid. Could be. I've wined and dined with kings, I have. You can tell, can't y'?

MIKE: Oh, deffo.

FRANK: So there y'are – a Mercedes is nothin' special to me. (FRANK *takes a bunch of keys out of his three-hundred-pound purple suit.*)

FRANK: Bernard here will attend to you. I've got one or two little . . . problems to sort out. You know. (*He opens the door.*)

MIKE: Not really, no, but incidentally, what *do* you do here, Frank?

FRANK: Nothing. (*Winks*) I'm a great one for delegatin', me. Anyway, I'll catch up with you later. See how you . . . manage.
(*He goes into the dim corridor leading from the door, and we see another door is at the end of the corridor. But we see no more.*)

MIKE: . . . You know, not everything here meets the eye.

BROKEN NOSE: Ah y' get them at the door, Boss. Usually after eleven o'clock, full of ale an' lookin' for a fight.
(MIKE *stares blankly at him.*)
They won't look you in the eye neither.

MIKE: (*Finally*) There is no answer to that.

BROKEN NOSE: Oh I dunno, I've got a few up me sleeve, things like 'fuck off before I give y' brain damage' . . . things like that.

MIKE: Of course, of course. I can see you're going to be a constant source of help and encouragement, Bernard.

BROKEN NOSE: Bernárd.

MIKE: Ahhh.

BROKEN NOSE: I was in the French Foreign Legion, y'see.

MIKE: Oh well, now that you tell me – (*He turns towards the double doors.*)

BROKEN NOSE: Er yeah, but listen, Boss, can I give you a piece of advice?

MIKE: Is this . . . really urgent?

BROKEN NOSE: Well, not yet, no, but I'm in charge of outside as well, an' I think you should know that no vehicle in like

24

recent memory has sort of ever survived longer than
half an hour in the car park because the kids around here
are savages and –

MIKE: Say no more. (*He turns away from the double doors and
moves towards the doors leading out of the club.*)
And if I'm not back in ten minutes, don't call me 'Boss' any
more, all right?
(BROKEN NOSE *nods.*)
By the way, what time do you . . . we open?

BROKEN NOSE: *Not yet.*
(MIKE *goes out.* BROKEN NOSE *closes the door. Gathers his
thoughts together.*)
. . . He won't last long.
(*He nods wisely to himself.*)

INT. THE MAIN HALL OF THE TWELFTH OF JULY MEMORIAL
CLUB.
*The bar is open. Drinks are on the table. Cigarette smoke lies heavy.
There is a gathering of* ORANGE LODGE *and* PROTESTANT
*pensioners sitting at tables surrounding the stage. Some react more
exuberantly than others to the music, as the twelve-piece veteran
band, to a man with a cigarette each in their mouths, finish playing
'Derry Walls'. The band are all men in their mid-sixties plus,
wearing a sash, a stiff peaked beret, dressed in dark suits, and
playing either an expensive matching accordion or a single drum of
varying size. A couple wear wigs. So do some of the men in the
audience. They often wear pork-pie hats.*
BILLY *steps forward, holding a stiff whiskey. He commands an
immediate respect and authority.*

BILLY: Ladies and gentlemen – the Veterans of the Southern
Cross Memorial Band.
(*Applause*)
And welcome, one and all: those we see every night, and
those who we . . . don't.
(BILLY *just glances across to* MR *and* MRS O'GORMAN, *but his
voice registers no insult. They can't hear him clearly anyway.*)
. . . Those who are regulars and those from our other
lodges in the city. And for those who don't know me, I'm
Billy McCracken.

(*Cries of* ''Course we know you, Billy Boy', *etc.*)
I was the grand master of this lodge, and now I'm a
pensioner. I'll talk no more, we have no time. But before
we go, a toast. Ladies and gentlemen, raise your glasses to
the Queen.
(*They all stand.* MRS O'GORMAN *struggles to her feet.*
Loudly.)

MRS O'GORMAN: Who?

MR O'GORMAN: The Queen.

MRS O'GORMAN: Oh, that's all right then, I'm not standin' up
for no soddin' gunmen, you tell him that, George.

ALL OF THEM: The Queen.

BILLY (*Drily*) Thank you, Martha, I'm glad to see you don't
change from year to year.
(*As they all sit down again, we see the* ULSTERMAN *on a pay*
phone at the back of the hall. Someone smashes a glass as they
sit down. It is enough to make the ULSTERMAN *jump violently.*
He slams down the phone.
People are now standing, putting their coats on, finishing their
drinks, preparing to go outside.
The Southern Cross veterans begin to pick up their drums in
anticipation.
The ULSTERMAN *slams the phone down again and follows*
them as they go out into the cold night air.)

EXT. CHARLESTON CLUB. NIGHT.
One of the steel shutters is coming off. BROKEN NOSE *and the other*
BOUNCER DOORMAN *struggle with it. Mainly because of* BROKEN
NOSE'*s lack of co-ordination/interest.*

BROKEN NOSE: . . . Not yet, not yet . . . cryin' out loud,
Knobby, it looks as though we're open . . .
(MIKE *opens the double doors. Beyond is the kind of place that*
has cost a lot of money to ruin. A woman's voice is heard
singing 'Blue Bayou'. Unaccompanied. MIKE *stops and looks*
towards the stage.
'*Blue Bayou' is just finishing. The singer,* CHERYL, *introduces*
the next song. Attempting the plastic sophistication of the likes
of Dolly Parton. MIKE *watches, alone, from the shadows of the*
doorway.)

CHERYL: . . . Thank you, thank you, you're so kind, and it's really wonderful to be back here again so soon after Caesar's Palace, and for my next number, I'd like to sing a song made famous by my old friend and confid . . . confide . . . companion, why he's almost like a daddy to me, Mr Ray Charles . . . well, he would be except he's black, but . . . anyway thank you, thank you . . . (*Holds up her hands modestly*) . . . it's a tune I'm sure you'll all know. (*Turns to 'The Orchestra Leader'*) Thank you, Max . . .
(CHERYL *starts singing 'Born To Lose'. With pathos and warmth. It is, for* MIKE, *almost shelter from the storm. He approaches the stage as she sings. Till she notices him. And stops immediately. And tries to see who it is.*)
Oh frig! . . . Who is it? I was just . . . (*She tries, unsuccessfully, to put the microphone back on the stand, drops the mike, knocks the stand over, trips over the wire, picks the stand up. We see the stand in her hand, the three prongs at the base facing* MIKE.) Oh look, the Isle of Man! . . . Are you the singer?

MIKE: Nah, the manager.

CHERYL: The singer's manager?

MIKE: Just the manager.

CHERYL: I don't get it.

MIKE: That's about par for the course. Y' not related to the bouncer, are y'?

CHERYL: If I am, he hasn't told me. (*She picks up some display cards and a small ground plan off the stage floor. Begins to walk towards the tables.*) What do you manage?

MIKE: To keep alive. Just about. Body an' soul's another matter.

CHERYL: (*Doubtfully*) Oh. Yeah . . .

MIKE: And you, what do you do here?

CHERYL: I help. Yeah . . . (*She places a card on a table.*)

MIKE: Well, that's a . . . (*Waves his hands about*) that's no threat to the Trades Description Act.

CHERYL: Yeah. If you say so . . . I've gotta go now. (*She focuses on his suit bag.*)

MIKE: And help.

CHERYL: Yeah. I help the chef. You know, the cook. And

things. And I put the cards on the tables. Y'know –
(*Reads*) 'Kirby Over 60s Club', 'The Runcorn Living Dead'
. . . Singers have them bags, y'know. Yeah. They have
their velvet jackets in them. And their trousers.

MIKE: I just keep me sandwiches in mine.

CHERYL: You takin' the piss out of me?

MIKE: No, no, it's . . . you like singing?

CHERYL: Yeah. Singin's the best. I love singin'. It makes me
feel like. Sort of. (*She glances down, embarrassed. Reads the
top card she has in her hand.*) Oh – hey, we've got the
soddin' Orange Lodge in too tonight. I hate the Orange
Lodge, do you? We all do in our house. It runs in the
family. (*She grins to herself.*) Well, I know who'll be gettin'
fed last tonight.

MIKE: I er . . . enjoyed it. The singing.

CHERYL: (*Who has a thousand ways of saying 'Yeah'*) Yeah?

MIKE: Honest.

CHERYL: Oh that's nice, 'cos it gets on everyone else's tits. (*She
walks away. Suddenly begins to run.*) Oh Christ, me soddin'
roasties!

(*She races away towards the kitchens.*

MIKE *slowly walks towards the doorway leading to the rear of
the club, where his manager's office is situated.*

*As he does so, some of the bar staff drift in from behind the long
'Black Bottom' Bar.*

*Someone flicks on the 'make you look ten years older and yellow'
fluorescent lighting that perhaps runs the length of the bar.*)

EXT. ST COLUMBA'S CLUB. NIGHT.
The CATHOLIC *fancy dress party are leaving their club. And head
towards the coach to take them away.*
LAUREL *and* HARDY, SUPERWOMAN, THE BLIND BOXER
(*Paddy Burke*), *a* FRENCH ONION SELLER, LITTLE BO-PEEP,
QUEEN ELIZABETH THE FIRST, SIR FRANCIS DRAKE, TWO
APES, QUASIMODO, FRED ASTAIRE *and* GINGER ROGERS,
SHIRLEY TEMPLE, SHIRLEY BASSEY, SHIRLEY WILLIAMS
(*joke*), CHARLIE CHAPLINS, SCARLETT O'HARA *and* RHETT
BUTLER, DONALD DUCK, YOGI BEAR, GRACIE FIELDS,
GEORGE FORMBY, OLD MOTHER RILEY, ADOLF HITLER *and*

many others. Last to come out is a man dressed as a priest. He is talking to a man dressed as WILD BILL HICKOCK. *But no Davy Crockett and West Indian limbo dancer.*

They approach their coach. In some high spirits.

PADDY BURKE *is in mid-manic-flight.*

PADDY BURKE: Oh aye, yeah, they wanted to give me a dog, a soddin' dog, I said sod off with y' soddin' dog, what do I want a dog for, I was a soddin' burglar, don't talk to me about soddin' dogs. (*Laughs. Stops abruptly*) I knew they were there, Tony, y'know, I could sense it, sod a dog f' sense with me around, I wish y'd seen me –

TONY BONAPARTE: I know, so –

PADDY BURKE: I've been in trainin' f' the likes of them, waitin' for them, darin' the bastards to make a move, feel that, go on, feel that – (*Flexes his right biceps.*) Like rock that. Rock. I ask y', has this body changed, Tony, has it?

TONY BONAPARTE: Only –

PADDY BURKE: You remember this body, don't y'?

TONY BONAPARTE: 'Course I do, Paddy. I never missed a fight.

PADDY BURKE: Riley in 'thirty-eight? Third round knock down.

TONY BONAPARTE: (*Quietly*) Apart from when I was in jail, Paddy.

PADDY BURKE: Y' know, I felt just like Charles Bronson before. Out on the streets of New York. Have you ever been to New York, Tony?

TONY BONAPARTE: No.

PADDY BURKE: Neither have I.

(TONY BONAPARTE *slips his hand inside his jacket.*)

TONY BONAPARTE: I haven't even been to France.

PADDY BURKE: What's that got to do with it?

(*The* PRIEST *at the front stands up. Looks around. Sees two empty seats. Looks at his list. Then at his watch. Reluctantly approaches the driver.*)

DRIVER: Bloody good that, pal.

PRIEST: . . . What?

DRIVER: Y' fancy dress. Cracker.

PRIEST: It's not fancy dress . . . We'd better be –

(*The* PRIEST *stops and looks out of the coach. From inside the coach we see a police Rover 3500 enter the social club car park and approach the coach at a speed designed to impress someone. The* POLICE DRIVER *and front seat passenger hustle around to the rear passengers' sides of the car.*
And BARBARA, *the West Indian limbo dancer, and* RONNY, *alias Davy Crockett, step out.*
RONNY, *donning his Davy Crockett hat, is still far from impressed, and is mouthing off and pointing as he walks away.*
BARBARA *walks on ahead to the coach. Determined to make a grand entrance.*)
BARBARA: You'll never guess what's happened to us!

INT. MANAGER'S OFFICE. CHARLESTON CLUB. NIGHT.
The room is littered with junk, empty wine bottles, crates of empty ale bottles, a cardboard box with 'First Aid' handwritten on it, bunches of keys on all surfaces, an iron, the 'Best of Max Bygraves' LP, money bags, a good quality cassette player chained to the wall. Tired photographs of previous artistes.
MIKE *is at a desk, sitting down, having changed into his formal night club manager's apparel. He is staring at the poster for tonight's show. No real information on it, certainly no mention of a Fancy Dress, but obviously aimed at pensioners.*
A knock on the open door. It is Bernard of the BROKEN NOSE. *And sudden fluster.*
BROKEN NOSE: Er hey you, Boss, er can y' come here. Please. Quickly.
MIKE: Trouble?
BROKEN NOSE: Not yet, but it's not 'not trouble', if y'know what I mean.
MIKE: Not yet.
(MIKE *stands and approaches the door. They walk towards the back of the bar area as they talk.*)
BROKEN NOSE: I know y' new an' that, so I rang Frank but he said it was your compartment. In no uncertain half terms.
MIKE: Good old Frank.
BROKEN NOSE: It's one of the turns, Boss.
MIKE: Y' can call me 'sir' if y' want.
BROKEN NOSE: All right sir, but wait till y' see these. Jesus

31

Christ, Mr McCarthur must have gone off his fuckin'
cake . . .
(*They approach the back of the bar.*)

INT. ORANGE LODGE HALL. NIGHT.
People are putting on coats and leaving the hall.
BILLY *is standing checking on everyone.*
One of the men greets BILLY *with an affable threat of hitting him
in his ample stomach.* BILLY *shields his stomach with his right arm,
slaps the man across the face lightly with his left hand, then quickly
'punches' the man in his stomach with his right fist. All with a speed
of movement that gives a lie to* BILLY'S *age and health. All good
natured. Except to* MRS O'GORMAN, *who has been watching.*
MRS O'GORMAN: Is he hitting people again, George?
MR O'GORMAN: No. He's had to stop. (*Quieter. Just*) He's been
    very ill.
MRS O'GORMAN: He was a very violent person when he was
    young . . . Even when he wasn't young.
BILLY: (*Loudly. Irritated but controlled*) Why don't you tell the
    whole bloody hall, Martha O'Gorman?
MRS O'GORMAN: (*Sweetly*) Is he talking to us, George?
BILLY: Y' only here cos it's a free night out, the pair of y'.
    Never see hide nor hair of y' otherwise. Where were y' on
    the Twelfth of July, hey?
MRS O'GORMAN: I have terrible trouble marching these days,
    Billy McCracken, and I never could bring myself to shout
    'Fuck the Pope' in public.
    (*There is some laughter in the hall.* BILLY *half smiles.*)
BILLY: (*Mouths silently*) Piss off, y' daft old cow.
MRS O'GORMAN: But I can lip read.
    (*Pause.*)
MR O'GORMAN: Very good, Martha . . . The one good thing
    about bein' old is that y' can say absolutely anything you
    want. To anyone y' want. And it doesn't matter at all.
    (*Pause*) An' y' know why, cos nobody ever listens to y'.

INT. THE FOYER OF THE CHARLESTON CLUB.
BROKEN NOSE, MIKE *and the* SILENT BOUNCER. *Facing 'Not
not trouble, not yet'. But soon. Standing in the doorway are a group*

32

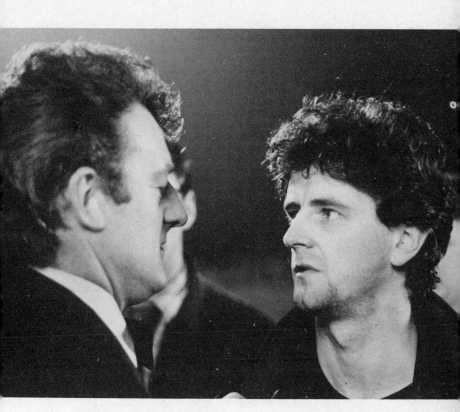

*who combine anarchy, lack of taste, the ugliest aspects of the very
latest fashion, integrity, obscenity and an inability to acknowledge
that rhythm plays any part in music.*
They are all in full flight.

BROKEN NOSE: (*Pointing at* MACKER) – and don't call me
   bollocks!

MIKE: Look, lads, first of all, what are y', an' what exactly are y'
   doin' here?

LEADER: We're the band.

BROKEN NOSE: Not yet y' not.

MIKE: Have y' got a confirmation card?

MACKER: No, but I've got me first holy communion certificate.
   (*He thinks he is sidesplitting. His* LEADER, *a studious boy in
   glasses, ignores him, shows* MIKE *a confirmation card.*)

LEADER: All right, Macker.

33

BROKEN NOSE: Can y' do Glen Miller?

MACKER: Y' mean fly off in the fog?

BROKEN NOSE: You'll fuckin' fly in a minute.

MIKE: All right, fellers, no offence meant, but there's been a mistake made – there's nothin' down for y' here – it's as simple as that – there'll be four hundred people in here tonight, an' every single soddin' one of them'll have a bus pass an' a pension book. They'll want to get legless, have a nice dance, a few laughs, lots of bingo an' a singsong at the end, an' if they're really adventurous, someone'll ask y' t' play 'Blanket On The Ground'. Right? Now, be honest, is that you?

MACKER: We don't do bingo.

MIKE: Oh hey, lad, when God give you teeth, he spoilt a good arse.

MACKER: I'll have two kebab an' chips, waiter.

BROKEN NOSE: (*Looking at* MACKER'*s neck*) I'm glad you come, I haven't seen a tide mark in ages.

MACKER: I fuckin' hate bouncers.

MIKE: All right, *all right*, now listen, who booked you in here?

LEADER: I dunno, do I? If you're the manager, you booked us in.

MIKE: I'm the manager now, but I wasn't then. I'll have to . . . sort this. (*Looks towards the door marked 'Private'*.)

LEADER: Look, we want t'play. We wanna play.

MIKE: All right.

(*Turns to* BROKEN NOSE) Tell Frank to be in my office in ten minutes.

BROKEN NOSE: Who me – I can't tell –

MIKE: *Tell him.*

INT. THE CATHOLICS' COACH. NIGHT.

Half- and quarter-bottles of spirits are beginning to appear in several quarters. Singing has commenced. Laughter abounds. Apart from the back seat . . .

PADDY BURKE: The trouble is, y' see, the trouble is that when we were kids, if we stepped out of line, we got battered. Anyone could batter y' then. An' not only that, you could batter anyone. We battered the Orange Lodge, they tried to batter us, we both used t' batter the Chinks an' the niggers, an' then the police battered the lot of us, though nobody could batter anyone better than I could batter them, that's right that, isn't it, Tony? But nowadays, nobody batters any bugger, not unless they've got a Stanley knife and fifteen mates, or fifty years' advantage, an' nowadays, nobody believes any bugger, nobody listens to any bugger, and the kids don't give a bugger. There's no values, there's no respect, there's no decency that I can see, and one thing I hope is that I put those two little bastards in intensive care. I hope they never walk again.

TONY: Yeah, dead right, Paddy.

(MRS CAREY *and* WINNIE *sitting next to each other.*)

MRS CAREY: . . . It's a wig, Winnie, 'course it's a bloody wig, he was as bald as a billiard ball at my John's funeral, how can he have hair now?

WINNIE: (*Looking*) What about a Hair Transport?

MRS CAREY: Y' mean Pickfords?

WINNIE: Whoever . . .

(MRS CAREY *looks out of the window.*)

MRS CAREY: Aahhh, look at those poor gets, broken down . . .

WINNIE: Ah, I know, what a shame, on a night like tonight . . .

(*From their viewpoint, a minibus. Broken down on a hill. Steam rising from the front.*)

. . . Still, it's a nice wig. It sort of matches the memory of his hair, doesn't it?

EXT. MINIBUS FOR THE INFIRM. NIGHT.

The broken down minibus. A glimpse, no more, of a very aged passenger or two.

One voice is heard.

YOUSEE: You see you see you see you see you see you see you see . . .

(*The minibus driver. Fifty and fat. And a master of philosophy.*)

WARDEN: Do you know what hypothermia is?

MINIBUS DRIVER: You mention hypothermia again to me . . .

35

WARDEN: All I'm saying is do you realize what can
    happen . . .
MINIBUS DRIVER: (*Flatly*) Look son, I'm like Stirling Moss
    used to be. I'm only the driver. Now, If I'd have hit a
    petrol tanker on the wrong side of the road, doin'
    eighty-five miles an hour, an' we'd all been burnt to
    buggery, you might have due cause for comment, but
    otherwise, all I know is that it won't go. *All right?*
WARDEN: (*Flatly*) Yes, but – I've got twelve old people freezing
    to death. (*Points back towards the bus.*)
MINIBUS DRIVER: I'm going to apply the comprehensive
    emergency procedure as laid down by the firm. For events
    such as these.
WARDEN: . . . And?
MINIBUS DRIVER: I'm goin' find a phone. Have you got
    tenpence, please?

EXT. A MAIN ROAD, DUAL CARRIAGEWAY. TRAFFIC LIGHTS.
TRAFFIC. NIGHT.
*The Orange Lodge bus draws to a halt. Waits for the lights to
change.*
The interior. Focus on BILLY *and the* ULSTERMAN.
ULSTERMAN: I'll stay in the toilets when we get there, Billy,
    just come out to use the phone . . . It might be a good
    idea after all, all this, y'know, safety in numbers, who's
    going to be lookin' for me with – suffering Jesus – (*Looks
    out of the window. Double takes*) – with . . . Would y' look
    at that!
    (*Pulled up alongside them, inevitably, is the coach carrying the*
    CATHOLICS *in fancy dress.*
    *A slow burn of recognition follows. People standing up on the
    Orange Lodge coach to look across. Names mentioned, then
    called. Jeering and laughter. The accordionists blast out 'The
    Sash . . .'*
    *The Catholics do not have the same rapture, although they too
    share the same recognition. An ape tries a V sign.* WILD BILL
    HICKOCK *draws his gun and points it at the coach. As it
    happens, directly at the* ULSTERMAN.)
    Fuckin' hell, he's got a gun! (*Throws himself down. And
    across* BILLY. *His hand already going suspiciously into his
    inside pocket.*)

BILLY: 'Course he has, he's a cowboy, y' soft get.
(*The Orange Lodge coach begins to pull away slightly as the lights change.*
But not before PADDY BURKE *stands and walks down the aisle in the Catholic coach, waving his stick, in his boxing gloves. And* BILLY *recognizes him. And the hatred, long dulled, flickers to life.*)
. . . Paddy Burke. Paddy Burke! (*He stands up.*) . . . Oh, sod it.
(*He sits down again.*
Very few others are sitting with him. They have the taste. There are cries of 'There's Paddy Burke!' 'The bastard!' And demands for BILLY *to see him. We should be aware that* PADDY BURKE *and* BILLY MCCRACKEN *once meant a lot to each other. One way or another.*
MR *and* MRS O'GORMAN *remain suitably unimpressed by the proceedings in their coach.*)
MRS O'GORMAN: Never left the playground, George, never left the bloody playground!

INT. OUTSIDE THE MANAGER'S OFFICE. CHARLESTON CLUB. NIGHT.
MIKE *walks into his office, straight into* FRANK, *standing in the doorway to* MIKE's *office.* CHERYL *follows, her presence giving an extra edge . . .*
FRANK: Well?
MIKE: Y'd better tell me what's going on.
FRANK: Why?
MIKE: 'Cos I want to know, that's why.
FRANK: It's not a good enough reason, I'm afraid. Sorry.
MIKE: It's good enough for me.
FRANK: I must have higher standards than you then. (FRANK *moves close to* MIKE. *Macho man in action . . .*) There's nothin' goin' on here that has anything to do with you. And for that be grateful.
(*Both men stare at each other. Unblinking.*
Enter BROKEN NOSE. *Through the manager's office.*)
BROKEN NOSE: I've been lookin' for y' everywhere, Boss, excuse me, Frank, but I'd like the Boss – him like – to

come out here a minute. Please. Now. It's the car park,
Boss. Hello, Cheryl.

(MIKE *takes one last look at* FRANK. *Turns and goes with*
BROKEN NOSE.)

EXT. THE CAR PARK, CHARLESTON CLUB. NIGHT.
Two coaches parked. The CATHOLICS *have just arrived.*
As the CATHOLICS *step down from their coach, they are 'greeted' by*
the massed ranks of many of the ORANGE LODGE *coach party,*
particularly by the VETERANS *in a swirl of celebration, voices and*
accordions.
BILLY *is there, but determinedly not prominent. The* ULSTERMAN *is*
hidden at the back, looking behind and around.
The CATHOLICS, *cut off from the club, come off the bus and begin*
to group together, their comments lost in the noise from the ORANGE
LODGE, *and their baitings:*

ORANGE VOICES: . . . Go ahead, then, go on, give us a song, seeing as y've been let out for the day . . . come on, y' Fenian fuckers, sing something . . . y' can't, y' can't, y've got no songs of y' own . . . (*A brief chorus*) 'No songs, no songs, no songs, no songs . . .' . . . Y' never have had an' y' never will . . . go on then, sing one of ours . . . come on, give us *something*! 'Carolina Moon' 'll do . . . who dressed you to come out tonight . . .

(*Then* PADDY BURKE *gets off the coach, stick waving, red-faced, with a neck like gas bottles. Bursting. And marching forward. The* PRIEST *makes one attempt to control him.*)

PRIEST: Please, Paddy, my son, not –

PADDY BURKE: Fuck off, Father.

(PADDY *marches at the* ORANGE LODGE, *stick swishing. Reaches them. There is silence, save for the odd mumbled insult.*) Billy McCracken! Billy McCracken! I know you're there. I

want you, Billy McCracken! We have unfinished business,
Billy McCracken.

(BILLY. *The people around him. They want some business.*
They expect it from BILLY, *even at the age of sixty-eight. One*
or two whisper and nudge him. The VETERANS *at the front*
with their accordions make way for him.

BILLY *stays where he is. Finally half-laughs, and shakes his*
head.)

BILLY: Not tonight, I have too much on my mind.

(*The* CATHOLICS *have something to celebrate.* PADDY BURKE
especially, as the ORANGE LODGE *look muted.*)

PADDY BURKE: Oh no, tonight, Billy McCracken. Tonight!

BILLY: Not tonight. Or any other night.

(*The* VETS *close in around* BILLY, *and fly into 'The Sash', but*
the CATHOLICS *enjoy* PADDY's *small victory.*

MIKE *and* BROKEN NOSE *are behind them at the Charleston*

Club doorway. Looking in some disbelief. As some of the ORANGE LODGE *begin to drift away, led by* MRS O'GORMAN.)

MIKE: What are they doing here in fancy dress?

BROKEN NOSE: . . . Maybe they followed the other coach.

(*And then they see, approaching the club doors, a tall angular young man,* ROSCO DE VILLE, *looking like a Modigliani portrait, with a strong hint of disorientation about him. He is carrying a rabbit hutch, a large box with air holes, which produces the occasional bird noises, and suit bag. Plus top hat. He looks hesitantly at the bedlam now subduing slightly in the car park, then even more hesitantly at* MIKE, *nods quickly at* BROKEN NOSE, *and moves into the club. Looks behind himself once to see if they are watching him. They are. He hurries through the double doors. Getting his rabbit hutch caught in the doors.*

MIKE *and* BROKEN NOSE *exchange glances.*)

Rosco De Ville.

MIKE: And . . . ?

BROKEN NOSE: I don't know what's going on, Boss. I don't. He was only here a fortnight ago. More's the pity.

MIKE: Died?

BROKEN NOSE: Died! We held a requiem mass for him.

(MIKE *laughs. Genuinely if despairingly.* BROKEN NOSE *is delighted. Laughs with* MIKE. *Stops instantly as he sees the* ORANGE LODGE *moving towards them. With music. With* MRS O'GORMAN *painfully in the lead.* MR O'GORMAN *fast approaching.*)

MR O'GORMAN: (*Going past*) Twelfth of July Memorial Hall, plus musical accompaniment, and at least one former terrorist.

(BROKEN NOSE *steps in front of the* VETERANS *carrying accordions.*)

BROKEN NOSE: Hey you. Gentlemen. No musical instruments in here. By order.

FIRST VET: (*Belligerently*). The only orders I listen to are 'Last Orders'.

MIKE: Y'll listen t' these, old son, or y' won't get y' first order in.

(MIKE *smiles pleasantly at them.*
One of the VETS *starts 'The Sash' again.*
BILLY *moves towards him and puts his hand over the accordion keys. The* VET *pushes his hand away.* BILLY *grabs it. Angrily.*)

BILLY: You heard the boy, we're to enjoy ourselves, that's all.

ACCORDION VET: Yeah, it's a pity we didn't enjoy ourselves in the car park.

BILLY: Put them away – back in the coach, go on.

(*As the* VETERANS *reluctantly obey* BILLY'S *orders,* MIKE *nods at* BILLY, *who barely responds. Mainly because he hears* PADDY *as the* CATHOLICS *approach.*)

PADDY BURKE: Billy! Billy Boy!

(MIKE *looks out. Sees forty-eight fancy dress costumes walking his way.*)

MIKE: They're coming here . . .

BROKEN NOSE: I am *not* phoning Frank.

(*As the* ORANGE LODGE *move through the double doors into the club proper,* MIKE *steps forward to the front entrance.* BROKEN NOSE *edges behind him.*)

MIKE: 'Evening, ladies and gentlemen, hope you don't mind me asking you, but have you got the right club?

MRS CAREY: 'Course we have, what d' y' think we are? Soft?

MIKE: No, no, not at all, but we weren't . . . (*Indicates their costumes*) . . . I mean, this is the Charleston Club. Madam.

MRS CAREY: And this is St Columba's Roman Catholic Social Club. Pensioners' piss-up. (*Some laughter*) Here's our card, young man, we're expected. (*She holds her card out to him, mock formally.*)

MIKE: But as far as I know, we weren't planning a fanc . . .
(*He reads the card. Including 'Fancy Dress Competition. First prize, a ten-days cruise for two'.*
MIKE *looks at* BROKEN NOSE, *who is laboriously mouthing the words. Gets to the 'Fancy Dress' part. Looks at* MIKE. *Shrugs every part of his body and face quietly. Edges away again.*)
Fanc . . . Fancy that.

MRS CAREY: Satisfied?

PADDY BURKE: Y'd better had be. (*To* BONAPARTE) What's happening, Tony?

TONY BONAPARTE: He doesn't seem to want to let us in.

PADDY BURKE: What! Where is he?

MIKE: No no! Nothing of the sort. Welcome to the Charleston Club, the night is young, and –

PADDY BURKE: I hate that word. In fact, I hate the young.

MIKE: And no – er, and well, the year is old, and the night is yours.
(*Glances around for help.* BROKEN NOSE *cannot look at him.*)

MRS CAREY: Yeah, fine, great, but listen here, you, we're only payin' pub prices for our drinks, the turkey dinner better had be, and do you have a 'Happy Hour'?

MIKE: Every hour is happy here. Madam.

MRS CAREY: (*Bustling through*) Well, we won't get much sense out of him.
(*The others follow through.* MIKE *stands and watches them go. Looks at the card. Looks towards the door marked 'Private'.*)

43

Then he hears BROKEN NOSE.)

BROKEN NOSE: Oh no . . .

(*A taxi has stopped outside. Enter the* COMEDIAN/*Master of Ceremonies and his* BOYFRIEND. *Each carrying a suit bag, and determined to flaunt and send themselves and their sexuality up the moment they see anyone 'straight'. Particularly someone like* BROKEN NOSE . . .)

COMEDIAN: Oh Bernard! Bernard Bernard Bernard! Oh Bernard!

BROKEN NOSE: Oh buggery . . .

(*The* COMEDIAN *eyes up* MIKE *as he takes hold of his friend's hand.*)

COMEDIAN: Well, the prospects of a foursome, Martin . . . Mmmm, see you later, boys . . .

(*They whirl away towards the double doors. With peals of laughter.* MIKE *has barely noticed them. Is several miles away. Or wishing he was.*)

BROKEN NOSE: Shirtlifters. (*Pause*) Dinner mashers. (*Pause*) Faggots. (*Pause*) Arse bandits.

(*Pause. Finally*)

MIKE: Is the fur coat the comedian?

(BROKEN NOSE *nods. Pause.*)

BROKEN NOSE: Poofter. Pervert.

MIKE: Yeah yeah, but is he any good?

BROKEN NOSE: Nah, fuckin' awful.

(MIKE *looks at the door marked Private again.*)

MIKE: I . . . have had . . . enough . . . of this.

BROKEN NOSE: I'll go and er . . . I'll get the old folk settled. Shall I? (*Doesn't wait for an answer. Hustles away.*)

INT. CHARLESTON CLUB. NIGHT.

GINGER ROGERS *and* FRED ASTAIRE *are alone on the dance floor. Flaunting.*

We see that the ORANGE LODGE *party and the* CATHOLIC *party have been placed facing each other in four groups of twelve, on one side and four groups of twelve on the other, down the middle of the club.*

There is a gap between them of one table, for a dozen people. But still empty.

*Some semblance of a truce at the tables as some of the men are
fighting for drinks at the bar, others are ordering drinks from the
WAITRESSES, and others again are just glad of the rest.*

SUPERWOMAN CAREY *and* SHIRLEY WINNIE TEMPLE *look
across towards the* ORANGE LODGE *tables.* SUPERWOMAN *is
putting her glasses on.*

We see BILLY *framed by two* VETS, *one with moustache.*

MRS CAREY: What d' you think about those two, Winnie, either
side of Billy the Beast?

WINNIE: Not a lot. (*She peers more closely.*) Him on the left put
our Roger in the Children's Hospital.

MRS CAREY: Oh hey! That was nearly sixty years ago, girl.

WINNIE: I know, but me mother always said that was the reason
he molested people.

MRS CAREY: He can molest me any day of the week.

WINNIE: Our Roger's dead.

MRS CAREY: No, him with the moustache, the one who broke your Roger's skull, I always fancied him, but he was on the wrong side. What's his name again?

WINNIE: I only ever knew him as Hatchethead . . . But d' y' think they'll go for us, y' know . . . dressed like this?

(*A* WAITRESS *comes with the drinks for* MRS CAREY *and* WINNIE. *Two orange juices.*)

WAITRESS: Forty-four pence please.

MRS CAREY: Daylight robbery. Sixteen pence each in Tesco's.

(*She pays up exactly. The* WAITRESS *sulks away.* MRS CAREY *watches her go and then gets a bottle of Bacardi from out of her handbag. Pours two trebles for her and* WINNIE.)

This'll open y' legs, Winnie!

WINNIE: (*Flatly*) It'd do better if it opened me bowels.

(MOUSTACHE *and* CLEANSHAVEN, *flanking* BILLY. *They know the ladies fancy them. And exchange wry smiles.*)

46

CLEANSHAVEN: Still, great days they were though.

MOUSTACHE: Yeah . . .

BILLY: D' y' think?

CLEANSHAVEN: Oh aye! For you especially, Billy Boy! King of the Castle!

BILLY: Pity it got repossessed.

OTHER VET: Come on, Billy!

MOUSTACHE: Don't worry, Billy, there's enough of us here.

CLEANSHAVEN: We'll stand by you.

OTHER VET: And you beat him last time, don't forget that.

MOUSTACHE: More than anyone else has ever done.

BILLY: I want no trouble tonight.

MOUSTACHE: But if there is, we'll be there.

INT. CHARLESTON CLUB FOYER. NIGHT.

MIKE *approaches the Private door. Goes past the* FRENCH ONION SELLER *and* LITTLE BO-PEEP, *who are on the one-armed bandits, and will be there throughout the night.*

In the corner, back turned, head down, is the ULSTERMAN *on a pay phone. Waiting. He slams the phone down hard as* MIKE *goes past him.* MIKE *glances at him, disinterested. The* ULSTERMAN *smiles an apology, pats the arm of the phone gently, turns and walks a shade too quickly into the 'Stags' toilets.*

MIKE *stands in front of the door marked 'Private'. We hold. He begins to bang his fist on the door. And bang and bang.* LITTLE BO-PEEP *wins forty pence.*

Sound of a door being opened and closed at the end of the corridor. Footsteps and FRANK.

FRANK: All right, all right, f'Christs sake! (FRANK *opens the Private door.*)

MIKE: Talk to me. Now.

FRANK: Again?

MIKE: *Now.*

FRANK: (*Singing*) 'Now and again there are fools such as I . . .'

MIKE: (*Flatly*) It's 'now and then'.

FRANK: I know, I was improvising.

MIKE: Look you –

    (MIKE *prods* FRANK *in the chest with his finger.* FRANK *grabs it.*)

FRANK: Nobody does that to me.

MIKE: That's all right, 'cos I am nobody, noted for it, an' nobody should have to put up with this, an' therefore this nobody is givin' in his notice. As from fuckin' now!

FRANK: Ah, I'm terrible, me. I don't take no notice.

(*He goes to close the door and turns away.* MIKE *pushes at the door, grabs hold of* FRANK *and shoves him part way down the corridor.*)

INT. PRIVATE ROOM COMPLEX. NIGHT.

Throws himself after FRANK, *grabs him again, and hurls him at the far door.*

At which point, MIKE *reverts to being a coward. Immediately. And* FRANK *starts breathing through his nose. One of the most frightening sounds known to cowards. Believe me.*

And the door opens behind FRANK. *As* MIKE *begins to back away. And there is* ROSS *the real owner of the club. Immaculately dressed. He will never raise his voice.*

ROSS: Trouble?

FRANK: Soon.

MIKE: You bet.

(FRANK *laughs. There is a whine of pain from inside the room.* ROSS *quietly closes the door. Approaches* MIKE. *As* FRANK *slowly works his way around* MIKE *so that the Private door is covered,* ROSS *shakes* MIKE's *hand formally and gracefully.*)

ROSS: Hello, Michael. How goes the night?

MIKE: (*Flatly*) Y' didn't mention this in the job description.

ROSS: No, I know, I didn't, did I? All interviews are the same really though, aren't they – I mean, I lie to you and you lie to me. And everyone is on their very best behaviour.

MIKE: Unlike tonight. (*Glances behind himself towards* FRANK.)

ROSS: Exactly.

MIKE: Well, you're going to have to re-advertise, Mr Ross, 'cos y' see, I thought I was gonna manage your night club, not a friggin' asylum for the violently insane. I'm not qualified.

ROSS: Oh, but you are. Really you are. (*A scream of pain comes from inside the room. Followed by sobbing.* ROSS *sighs and shakes his head.*)

In fact, you're highly qualified. Let me show you . . .

(ROSS *opens the door to the room. Walks in.* MIKE *stays where he is.* FRANK *moves him.* MIKE *enters the room.*)

INT. PRIVATE ROOM. NIGHT.
A room with two doors.
Inside the bloodshed and the former manager, MCCARTHUR, *and two* HEAVIES *and the chair that the former manager is tied to.*
MCCARTHUR *is a mess. A bloody mess. No titillation nor suggestion that there is any romance in violence.*
ROSS: You see, I do think, despite our teething troubles, not to mention McCarthur's teething troubles, (*Sniggers*) I do really believe that you could be very happy here, no, really, but I think perhaps you should see what becomes of the . . . (ROSS *struggles for the correct expression.*)

49

FRANK: Brokenhearted?

ROSS: Don't be silly, Frank . . . no, the . . . consequences of one's actions. Yes. (*He is pleased with himself.*) That was almost certainly the mistake we made with this . . . little thief in the night.

(*Smiles all round. Except for* MCCARTHUR *and* MIKE.)

MIKE: Goodbye.

ROSS: Oh, you can't go yet. Not yet. We haven't had the floor show yet.

(*He tilts* MCCARTHUR's *chair back, and the former manager topples backwards to the floor.* FRANK *and the* TWO HEAVIES *have already moved behind* MIKE *to cover the door.* MIKE *turns to discover this. He turns back to see and hear* MCCARTHUR *crying, lying strapped to the chair, facing the ceiling.*)

FRANK: See, I told you he was going to sing.

MIKE: WHATEVER IT IS, I DON'T WANT TO KNOW!

(*A brief silence. Spoilt by sobbing.*)

ROSS: . . . There you are, Michael, I knew you were the right
man for me. With a perfect attitude. Head down, nose
clean, blinkered and honest. As well as possibly being a
little bit . . . scared.

MIKE: Ah, a fortune teller.

ROSS: No. Far from it. I am a businessman. I adopt the
principles of market forces and fear. Try charm at first by
all means, and then use terror. Robert here will vouch for
that.

MIKE: That's quite a philosophy you've got there, but –

ROSS: And I haven't finished yet. Because as I told you, and I do
wish you would listen, for your own sake . . . you can be
very happy here. Truly. (*Looks down*) He was happy here.
But he got spoilt. And now . . . we've spoilt him . . . We
can spoil you too. If you want. (*Jovially*) What do you say?

MIKE: Nah, no thanks, this is another world. I don't belong
here.

ROSS: Of course you don't. I wouldn't want you to be a part of
this . . . unpleasantness. Just run my little club for me, let
my . . . questionable money run through here, don't rob
too much off me, be nice to those with varicose veins who
come here, *and don't get too ambitious*. Now then, Mike,
whatever can be the problem?

MIKE: Forget it.

ROSS: Oh, come on, you can talk to me. You have to talk to me.
Call me Leonard, if you want . . .

MIKE: (*Finally*) Well, apart from discovering this torture
chamber here, I've got a group who can't play music, one
bad comedian plus boyfriend, a nervous breakdown calling
himself a magician, two coachloads of seventy-year-old
religious maniacs looking for a fight, and a fancy-dress
contest that nobody knew about – first prize, a ten-days
cruise for two.

(MIKE *flicks the card at* ROSS. ROSS *studies it, then looks to*
MCCARTHUR, *looks down at him.*)

ROSS: Did you do this, Robert? Did you?

(MCCARTHUR *nods upwards.* ROSS *laughs. Picks him and the
chair up as he talks.*)

ROSS: You booked in all the . . . rubbish and then sent out the

phoney fancy dress invitations? As a sort of farewell present? (*More reluctant nods from* MCCARTHUR.)
Bugger me sideways, Robert, you almost go up in my estimation. (ROSS *tips him up again.*) Almost. (*He turns his back towards* MIKE.) You give them the cruise, no problem – my travel agency'll sort them out – we do a good deal with Russian boats, Spanish food and a Turkish crew. The rest of the night is up to you.

MIKE: . . . And if I don't want to do it?

ROSS: Well, I hardly think you've got much option now, do you? I mean, TINA.

(MIKE *looks around. Who is Tina?*)

MIKE: . . . Tina?

ROSS: There Is No Alternative. And after all, Uncle Mike, Butlin's Red Coat, friend to the under-fives, failed artiste but nice man, nothing you do here should be too much for you. (*He puts his arm around* MIKE.) All you have to be is honest and warm. I like to see those qualities. I respond to them. Generously. (*Takes his arm away.*) Now, if you'll excuse me, we still have another six and a half grand to find, don't we Robert?

MIKE: . . . What happens if I walk out of here now and disappear?

ROSS: You mean, without trace?

(ROSS *walks towards a drinks cabinet. Back turned, he deliberates over a drink. The others stare at* MIKE.
MIKE *finally goes to the door.* FRANK *opens it for him. Pats* MIKE *on the head, ruffles his hair.*)

FRANK: There's a good boy.

(MIKE *goes out. The door closes behind him.*
We see MIKE *lean against the door. Puts his hands over his eyes. We hear another whine of pain from inside.*
MIKE *hurries down the corridor.*)

INT. MAIN HALL.
As we move across to PADDY BURKE *and* TONY BONAPARTE, *they are sitting next to* DAVY RONNY CROCKETT *and* BARBARA THE LIMBO DANCER.

PADDY BURKE: Have y' got that, Tony?

TONY: Yeah, it's a . . . good idea, smart thinkin', like. Even
things up. (*Points*) I'll go and sort of case the joint now.
(*Stands.*)

BARBARA: Oooohhhh. Oh hey.

PADDY BURKE: While y' at it, I'll have a brown over mild an' a
double Jamesons.

BARBARA: Oh!

RONNY: What is it?

PADDY BURKE: It's all right, Ronny, Tony's gettin' them in.
(TONY BONAPARTE *pulls a quiet face. Goes to move away.*)
An' make it exact. I want t' know exactly where it is.
(*As* TONY *goes, we focus on* RONNY *and* BARBARA.)

RONNY: But what is it, Barb?

BARBARA: Me chest is all hot.

RONNY: I'm not surprised, y' wearin' a pair of false tits, two
tonne of makeup, an y've had a quarter of a bottle of gin on
the bus. As well as all the stupid excitement.

BARBARA: No, but it is.

RONNY: Just breathe in. Go on. Nice an' easy.
(*She breathes in. Appears to begin to recover.*)
PADDY BURKE: (*Suddenly, madly*) Hey Billy Boy! I'm here,
Billy!
RONNY: (*Under his breath*) Oh friggin' Jesus . . . Is that better?
BARBARA: . . . A bit better. But y'know what I've forgotten,
Ronny.
RONNY: (*Eyes closed*) Y' haven't, have y'?
(*Opens his eyes and looks at her. She has.*)
. . . Just try an' relax f' ten minutes, hey?
PADDY BURKE: What's the matter, Billy?
(PADDY BURKE *makes chicken noises. Laughs. Searches for
his pint and drinks heavily. Bangs it down.* RONNY *takes his
hat off and throws it on the table. Glances at* PADDY.
BARBARA *breathes deeply on.*)

EXT. CHARLESTON CLUB. NIGHT.
MIKE *breathes deeply into the fresh air. Feels into his pockets.
Touches and takes out his car keys.
Someone is at his shoulder. It is* FRANK. *Looking over his shoulder.
At the car keys.*
FRANK: . . . 'It's not the leaving of Liverpool that grieves
me . . .'
MIKE: I wish I was funny. I wish I thought I was funny.
FRANK: Seriously though, Michael, don't go. Not now. It'd be
very foolish to go now.
MIKE: Y' can get used to threats, y' know.
FRANK: That was a promise.
MIKE: I'll think of something.
FRANK: I doubt it.
MIKE: *Don't* doubt it.
FRANK: But I do. I mean, y' couldn't sell y' house in time. An'
even if y' went far away, I wouldn't mind. I like holidays.
MIKE: *But I haven't done anything!*
FRANK: Yeah, I know, but these days witnesses to the crime are
often in as much danger as those what to whom the crime
has been done. To.
MIKE: (*Laughs*) Y' all right on one-liners, aren't y', but y' don't
half fall apart on long sentences.

FRANK: Don't be like that. Not when we're just about to be
friends. We can be good for each other. We can work
together. Me an' you.

MIKE: Really?

FRANK: 'Course we can. McCarthur was a fool.

MIKE: *But y' shouldn't get beaten t' shit just f' bein' a fool.*

FRANK: Oh, it was more than that. Y'see, he wanted it all for
himself. Whereas me an' you, now that we understand each
other, we can do it quietly and together. Believe me, there's
better ways of robbin' Mr Ross than the ones he came up
with. (FRANK *smiles generously and happily at* MIKE.) I'll
leave you with that thought, shall I? Instead of you having
to think of something. But don't stand out here too long,
y'll catch y' death . . . (FRANK *leaves him.*)
(*After an age,* MIKE *puts his car keys back into his pocket.*)

INT. OUTSIDE MIKE'S OFFICE. NIGHT.

MIKE *at the door to his room.* BROKEN NOSE *seated at his desk. A lighted cigar of some proportions in his mouth, the chair swinging. Phone in hand.*

There are dull sounds of conflict from the dressing-rooms.

BROKEN NOSE: . . . So Mr Parnell, I decided to become a comedian after I escaped from the Foreign Legion, an' hey listen, if y' can get a laugh in French, y' can get a laugh any –

    (*He turns and sees* MIKE, *as* MIKE *walks through.*)

MIKE: D' y' have an audition night here?

BROKEN NOSE: Er Tuesdays.

MIKE: I'll put your name down, with all the other dreamers, and don't hide the cigar, y' can have them. It's called theft normally, but here it's just called normal.

BROKEN NOSE: (*Getting up to follow* MIKE) Oh, er no, it was just . . . but, er, thanks, Boss . . .

    (*Takes the cigars as he goes.*) Everything all right with Frank?

MIKE: (*From outside*) No. *But it will be.* One way or another . . .

INT. CORRIDOR BY DRESSING-ROOMS. NIGHT.

The group playing. MIKE *and* BROKEN NOSE *listen too.*

LEADER: Y' finished, Macker!

MACKER: Finished? I haven't started yet . . . Oh aye, takin' our glasses off now, are we?

INT. FIRST DRESSING-ROOM. NIGHT.

MIKE *and* BROKEN NOSE *enter.* BROKEN NOSE *enjoying the importance that he thinks the cigar gives him. Smoke everywhere.*

MACKER: (*Turning away*) It's too late t' look hard, Duncan. In fact, it's impossible. Fuckin' students . . .

MIKE: If y' wanna fight, go to the stadium. Are y' on or not, lads? An' if you are, I want them dancin' not complainin'.

LEADER: Can y' give us a bit longer?

BROKEN NOSE: You lot need eternity. An' that wouldn't be long enough.

    (MIKE *and* BROKEN NOSE *go out.*)

MACKER: There's a musician talking.

INT. ROSCO'S DRESSING ROOM. NIGHT.
Through the doorway ROSCO DE VILLE. *He is dressed up, pacing nervously, talking to himself. His rabbit hutch is on the table. Next to his pigeons. And a glass of water.*
ROSCO: Good *evening*, ladies and . . . *good* evening, ladies and gentlemen. *Good evening!* Ladies and gentlemen. Good –
(*Sees* MIKE *and* BROKEN NOSE *staring at him.*)
Ah. Good evening. (*A table-tennis ball drops out of his sleeve.*) Rosco De Ville.
BROKEN NOSE: (*As if describing a disease*) Novelty act.
(CHERYL *at the doorway, joining the other two.*)
ROSCO: I do a bit of everythin' actually, but I'm worried about me rabbit. It's just sort of the highlight of me act, me rabbit.
MIKE: Sod y' rabbit, can y' sing country an' western?
ROSCO: Everythin' apart from singin', I should have said.
CHERYL: (*Quietly*) I can sing.
ROSCO: An', er, me rabbit's sick. A touch.
(*No answer.*)
(MIKE *and* BROKEN NOSE *exchange glances.* CHERYL *looks at the rabbit.* ROSCO *flicks his hand out. Produces a playing-card. Two more fall out of his cuff. He smiles. In a fashion.*)
MIKE: We'll put y' on in the middle. An' we'll have a vet standin' by.
(MIKE *turns to go. The others follow him.*)

INT. THE CHARLESTON CLUB.
MIKE *in bathroom mirror.*
MIKE: . . . Do something . . . *do* something . . . something . . . come on, do something . . . *do it* . . . Just for once . . . hey?

INT. THE CHARLESTON CLUB. NIGHT.
The 'Stags' toilet.
TONY BONAPARTE *is rechecking his measurements. Pacing between the toilet door and the light switch. Holds his hand out level. Then adjusts it to where the light switch is.*
BILLY *stands at the door, watching him.* TONY BONAPARTE *turns*

around and sees BILLY. *Starts to smile. Pathetically. Decides against going through the doorway. Moves to the urinals.* BILLY *follows him.*

BILLY: (*Quietly*) If you're thinking of assistin' in the plannin' of anythin' tonight, Tony Shitehawk Stavoni, you'd better think again. Nothing is to happen here tonight, d' y' hear me?

TONY BONAPARTE: (*With sickening geniality*) 'Course I do, Billy. Last thing on my mind.

BILLY: It will be, believe me.

(TONY BONAPARTE *scuttles out.* BILLY *moves down the toilets to the cubicles.* BILLY *half goes into a cubicle, comes out when they go to the urinal. Gets to the last cubicle, which is locked. Looks around. All clear. Knocks on the door. Knocks again.*)

(*Whispers*) Norman.

(*The door opens. We see the fully clothed* ULSTERMAN *and his almost empty bottle of whiskey.* BILLY *enters, closes the door.*)

What is happening?

ULSTERMAN: I can't get any answer.

BILLY: You mustn't stay here. There are things going wrong. Out there.

ULSTERMAN: The fucking Catholics! I can hear them in here. I want to go out there and fuckin' . . . (*He can barely cohere.*) . . . fuckin' . . .

BILLY: I have some money. With me.

ULSTERMAN: Fuckin' . . .

BILLY: Enough for a taxi to almost anywhere.

ULSTERMAN: Are you tryin' to get me caught, Billy? That's the first thing the police would have done – warned the taxis. No . . .

BILLY: I want you to go. If the police come here –

ULSTERMAN: That wouldn't be good. For the both of us, Billy, 'cos only you know I am here.

BILLY: The police will come if there is trouble. And trouble is brewin'.

ULSTERMAN: I'll phone again. In a while.

BILLY: Norman. Go away. I don't want you here . . . *I am scared!*

ULSTERMAN: You – scared. (*Shakes his head*) Don't be scared, Billy. Just think of your sweet daughter.

BILLY: But that is why I am scared. (*Points. Raises his voice*) If one finger is laid on her and her kin because of you – (*They are both aware of someone approaching the nearest cubicle. Almost freeze into still positions, like Tussaud's. The other person enters the cubicle. Etc. The* ULSTERMAN *leans in to* BILLY. *Whispers.*)

ULSTERMAN: Not because of me, Billy Boy, because of you. (*They look at each other. Finally* BILLY *opens the door and leaves.*)

INT. THE STAGE OF THE CLUB. NIGHT.

The COMEDIAN. *His death is almost complete. Few are listening to his death. Anyway, he has died before.*

MIKE, CHERYL *and* BROKEN NOSE *at the side of the stage.* MIKE *looks in some pain.* CHERYL *looks at his bum, and* BROKEN NOSE *looks delighted.*

COMEDIAN: (*Pointing to someone near the front*) Look at him, just look at him, misery – what! Been to a funeral today – waste of time him coming home, wasn't it? Give my love to Bing Crosby when you see him. If you don't laugh I'll stay on longer. You don't frighten me. Shut up or I'll set your pension books on fire. (*Laughs. No reaction. He looks towards* MIKE. *Who indicates him to wind up. Fast.* BROKEN NOSE *gives him the thumbs-up sign.*)

All right, eyes down for a full house!

(*He gets almost instant silence, then a fury of voices and searching for pens.*)

Just my little joke, ladies and gentlemen, still it was nice to get a bit of silence and attention once in a while, a few laughs'd help as well, now and then . . . I'll take a short break now while I go an' try an' kill meself, replenish your glasses, a magician's on next, thank you very much, I'd like to say, by the way, that you've been a good audience.

(*Takes the microphone slightly away from himself.*)

I'd like to, but I can't . . .

(*He bows to nothing. Walks away. Approaches* MIKE. *Savagely*) Fucking coffin dodgers.

INT. THE BODY OF THE HALL. NIGHT.
PADDY BURKE's *table*.
PADDY BURKE *and* TONY BONAPARTE. *Eventually,* RONNY *and*
BARBARA.
PADDY BURKE: Did it land anywhere?
TONY BONAPARTE: (*Not looking*) Direct hit . . . are y' sure y'
still want me to do it, the first one's by the door, the second
one's five paces straight, two to the –
PADDY BURKE: *You do it.*
(*No answer.*)
I'll have the same again. (*Taps glass.*)
TONY BONAPARTE: . . . Er what about havin' a kitty, hey? We
both –
PADDY BURKE: Just for the pair of us – don't be soft.
(TONY BONAPARTE *gives up and goes.* BARBARA *is not well.*
It is not funny.)
BARBARA: . . . I'm not well, Ronny.
RONNY: I know, I know. I'll take you home, get the pills.
BARBARA: But we'll miss . . . everything. The fancy dress and
everything.
RONNY: They don't have cruises in intensive care. Come on. We
might get back in time anyway . . .
(*He stands her up. She struggles to stand. They both begin to*
move away. PADDY BURKE *flaps around for* RONNY's *arm.*)
PADDY BURKE: Don't be long, Ronny. There's going to be
some fun here!
RONNY: Oh great, I'll er . . . But Barbara's not so –
PADDY BURKE: Fun!
(*It doesn't sound too much like 'fun'.*)
RONNY: (*Trying to go*) What makes y' think that?
PADDY BURKE: 'Cos I'm going to start it! Billy! Billy Boy! This
time!
(*He laughs joyously. Lets go of* RONNY. *To* RONNY's *relief.*
And as RONNY *and* BARBARA *make their way towards the*
exit, MIKE, BROKEN NOSE *and* CHERYL *are watching*
PADDY BURKE. *From the bar where* BROKEN NOSE *has*
invested more of MIKE's *money.* PADDY BURKE *flicks a beer*
mat in the general direction of the PROTESTANTS *and*
ORANGE LODGE. *Yet again.*)

MIKE: A Catholic.

CHERYL: Years of persecution. It's only because he's underprivileged.

(*As* MIKE *laughs, genuinely, they hear the crash of glass. Turn to the bar to see one of the* VETS *has been accidentally bumped by* OLIVER HARDY *at the bar. Broken glass on the floor.*

CHERYL *obeys her occasional instinct to 'help', goes towards the glass. The* VET *has hold of* OLIVER HARDY. *A couple more* VETS, *ciggies dangling, move towards them.*)

VET: 'Kin' Fenian – can't y' look where y' going?

HARDY: I didn't –

VET: Y' goin' to pay for them.

HARDY: I know I am. And if I was a bit fitter so would –

VET: What y' waiting for then?

(*The* VET *pushes* HARDY. *Hard.*)

CHERYL: Leave him alone, y' orange fart.

VET: Stay out of this. *Woman.*

(*The* PRIEST, *two* CHARLIE CHAPLINS, QUASIMODO, CAPTAIN BLIGH *and* RHETT BUTLER *move to* HARDY'*s side.*

The VETS *close in on each other.* PADDY BURKE *has heard trouble. He approaches.* MIKE *and* BROKEN NOSE *move in.* BILLY *approaches.*)

PRIEST: Please, gentlemen, the season of goodwill.

VET: There is no season of goodwill between us.

MIKE: There better had be tonight, 'cos otherwise, old as y' are, y'll still go out the door. Can you keep a grip of these, Father?

PRIEST: Do you want an honest answer?

MIKE: Don't bother. What about you?

BILLY: I can't keep a grip of myself these days, kid.

PRIEST: (*To* BILLY) You don't remember me, do you, Billy?

BILLY: . . . No.

PRIEST: (*Fingering his broken nose*) I remember you.

BILLY: (*To* MIKE) I'll do my best.

PRIEST: (*To* MIKE) But if I were you, I'd just call the police now and get it over with.

(BILLY *looks at him. The* PRIEST *joins* HARDY. MIKE *stares out.*)

MIKE: . . . Now there's an idea!

CHERYL: Yeah . . . What is?

(BILLY *walks away. Quickly.*)

MIKE: Nothing. Just that things could be warming up.

CHERYL: Gravy.

MIKE: Gravy?

CHERYL: I'm always doin' it, I've left me friggin' gravy on. (*She hustles off towards the kitchens.*)

EXT. THE ROAD LEADING FROM THE CHARLESTON CLUB. NIGHT.

RONNY *is looking for a cab.* BARBARA *is leaning against a wall. Suddenly* BARBARA *slides down the wall.* RONNY *rushes to her side. She is breathing irregularly, gasping.* RONNY, *clumsily and with difficulty, rips out the plastic breasts and starts to pound* BARBARA's *chest.*

BARBARA: I'm sorry, I'm sorry, I'm sorry.

(*A minibus last seen broken down is heading towards them, and the Charleston Club. It goes past. Slowly. Some steam rising from the front end.*

As the bus parks outside the club, it seems to give a sigh.)

INT. THE BODY OF THE HALL. NIGHT.

The disorder stopping.

As the PENSIONERS *see ten very elderly people in varying degrees of infirmity and physical disability arrive in their midst.*

The reactions of many of the pensioners. Of barely being able to look, hardly able to stop, looks of fear and loathing. As if a terrible future has arrived.

MIKE *and* BROKEN NOSE *are at the bar.* BROKEN NOSE *sees them first. His eyes following them.* MIKE *turns.*

MIKE: Listen, I want you to do something, Bernard, will you hold the . . .

(*Sees the* INFIRM) . . . hold the f . . . fuck.

(*The* INFIRM *struggle to be seated in the centre of the club, between the* ORANGE LODGE *and the* CATHOLICS.

Auxiliary nurse MRS MORGAN *has her arm around a weeping white-haired* BOBBY. *The rest of the* INFIRM *seem isolated from each other. One or two mutter and mumble.* BOBBY'*s body jerks into convulsive sobs. Inevitably but discreetly someone slobbers. We see the elderly man whose voice was heard in the broken down minibus mumbling 'You see, you see, you see, you see . . .'*

OLD BOBBY *is being held tight by* MRS MORGAN *who is fighting to keep patient.*)

MRS MORGAN: . . . Come on, Bobby . . . sssssshhhhhhh . . . there, there.

BOBBY: Where?

MRS MORGAN: Just stop crying, hey? It's a big night. Isn't it nice?

(BOBBY'*s sobbing continues unabated, reaching a childlike rage and fury.*)

MRS MORGAN: . . . Do you want to tell me what you're crying for, Bobby?

BOBBY: . . . I'm crying because I haven't got a mummy and a daddy.

(MRS CAREY *and* WINNIE TEMPLE.)

MRS CAREY: Oh, sweet Jesus. It shouldn't be allowed. They've got no right to be here. Like that. With us.

WINNIE: I know, it's a pity, isn't it?

MRS CAREY: . . . Have y' ever looked into the future, Winnie?

64

WINNIE: I had a dream once about the winner of the Grand
National . . . But it was the day after.
(MRS MORGAN *struggles to seat everyone. Looks for help, or
even service. The* OLD WAITRESSES *ignore her studiously.
Several of the* INFIRM *are dazed and in some difficulties. Some
slump head-down on to the table as soon as they are seated.*
BOBBY *stands up.* MRS MORGAN *sits him down.* BOBBY
stands up.
*Establish this; also some of the reactions from the others,
perhaps cutting into the above sequence.*
CHERYL *comes from the kitchens, approaching* MIKE *and*
BROKEN NOSE.
MR *and* MRS O'GORMAN, *holding hands. Tightly.*
BILLY, *flanked and flat. Looking at them.*)

BILLY: . . . Is this all there is?

MOUSTACHE: You should know, Billy, you booked us into this
shambles.

BILLY: No, I meant . . .
(MIKE *motions a drinking movement, nods to the bar.* CHERYL
copies him. BROKEN NOSE *goes to the bar.*)

MIKE: Get the drinks in, Bernard. . . . How old d'you think
they are?

CHERYL: Too old.

MIKE: Give us forty years, hey, girl? And there we'll be, spoilin'
everyone else's night.

CHERYL: Speak f' y' self.

MIKE: Greeted like a contagious disease. Is that all we've got to
look forward to? (*Glances at his watch*) Y' may as well go
out with a bang.

CHERYL: At The Third Stroke.
(MIKE *looks at her, looks back at his watch.*)
That's what we used to call me Gran. She'd had two, y' see.
At The Third Stroke. She drove me mother demented.
Worse than a baby at the end. Me an' our Tommy hated
her f' what she did to me mam. Used to sneak up behind
her and' kick her up the bum.

MIKE: She did that to your mother?

CHERYL: (*Flatly*) No, we did it to her . . . Still, she was a laugh
sometimes. Priest came to see her once, on one of the nights

65

when she was dying, asked her if she ever had any regrets
. . . an' she said, 'The only regret I've ever had, Father,
was that I never got enough dick.'

(MIKE *laughs.* CHERYL *looks slyly at him.* BROKEN NOSE
returns. As they drink, they look across towards the INFIRM.
BOBBY *is playing tug of war with* MRS MORGAN.)

MIKE: McCarthur doesn't deserve me . . .

CHERYL: Yeah, he wasn't very nice . . . Why, what are y' doin'
for him?

MIKE: Nothin' really. I'm doing it for myself. Bernard, tell the
comedian to disappear, but we'll pay him in full –

(BROKEN NOSE *smiles happily. Stops smiling happily as he
sees 'something' to the side of* MIKE.)

– get the magician ready for me, and if he . . .

(MIKE *sees* BROKEN NOSE's *face. Looks to his side.
We see* ROSCO DE VILLE *in full gear plus top hat. Standing
there. Total deadpan panic.*)

. . . dies.

ROSCO: (*Fast*) Er, excuse me, Mr Thingy, erm it's like this, I er
can't go on – (*Points off towards the stage*) – there. In front
of *them.* 'Cos. Like. Me rabbit. Y'know. (*Points up*) On me
head. It's the big point in me act, but it's had an accident.
(*The others look towards the top of his head. He lifts his hat.
We briefly see a rabbit crouched. And a very small brown
dribble by* ROSCO's *hairline.*
ROSCO *immediately drops his hat.*)
It's not me, it's me rabbit. (*He immediately produces a card
from the back of his hand as he talks. From his other hand silk
scarves appear.*) As you can see, I have been compared to
Paul Daniels. Only taller. With my own head of . . .
(ROSCO *goes to put his hand up to his head. Thinks better of
it.*) You don't have to pay me. Off. (*Turns away*) I
understand . . . It's tough at the top . . . (*He says the last
line bitterly. Takes his hat off his head and hurls it away.
Takes the rabbit off his head and throws that too. Anywhere.*)

MIKE: All right, throw the band straight on, an' if all else fails,
I'll get up there an' do a few numbers. Meanwhile –

BROKEN NOSE: *You?* I mean, you?

CHERYL: I knew you were a singer.

MIKE: Yeah, I'm glad y' used the past tense – go ahead,
Bernard.
(BROKEN NOSE *goes towards the stage area.*)
Look, do me a favour, Cheryl. (*Puts his arm around her
shoulder.*) Get that lot looked after, an' then get some food
out, the only chance we've got tonight is if we keep them
occupied. Go on. (*He tries charm.*) For me. Please.
CHERYL: Yeah.
MIKE: I said 'go on'.
CHERYL: Yeah, all right. Listen, d' you . . . fancy a fuck?
MIKE: . . . There's quieter ways of occupyin' them than that,
Cheryl.
CHERYL: Not now but –
(*He points at the kitchens. Turns her around and gently pushes
her away. She goes. He turns to go towards his office. Stops
and looks back at her as she walks away. Then goes.*)

INT. THE FOYER OF THE CLUB. NIGHT.
The ULSTERMAN *on the phone. And he gets through.*
ULSTERMAN: 'Would you like to come to the pictures tonight,
it's a war film.' . . . Don't say my name, how many times
do I have to tell you? . . . *Where have you been?* Both my
places of safety have gone here, I need to leave now . . . as
soon as possible. (*Glances at his watch.*) I'll be in the end
cubicle of the toilets in the Charleston Club on Stanley
Road . . . have y' got that . . . and make sure you're not
followed . . . Yeah.
(*He puts the phone down. Allows himself a thin grin. Moves
back towards the 'Stags' toilet.*
(*Passes the* WARDEN *and sweet* MATTHEW.)
MATTHEW: Thank you very much, Mr Richards, thank
you . . .

INT. A DOSS HOUSE OF THE FLAT. NIGHT.
One of the OLDER POLICEMEN *is using the phone.* TWO
desperately YOUNG ULSTER BOYS, *looking scared and sick.*
OLDER POLICEMAN: (*Fast*) Yeah – end cubicle, men's toilets,
Charleston Club, Stanley Road. Yeah. (*He throws the phone
down.*)

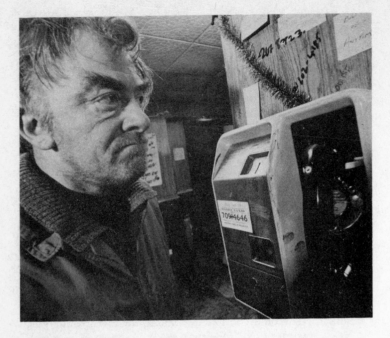

OTHER POLICEMAN: You're going to get twenty years for this, lads, an' y' know what, I'm glad.

OLDER POLICEMAN: Come 'head, I'm not fuckin' missin' this. (*Moves swiftly to the door, as the lads are hurled to their feet.*)

INT. THE MANAGER'S OFFICE. NIGHT.
Knocking on a door.
MIKE *on the phone. With a disguised effeminate voice.*

MIKE: (*Lisping*) Yes, that's right, officer, the Charleston Club, a man getting absolutely battered . . . no, I'm certainly not a crank . . . thank you.
(*He throws the phone down. Seals an envelope on his desk, puts it in his pocket. As someone tries again to open the door from the dressing room corridor. Knocks.*)

BROKEN NOSE: Boss . . . Boss . . .
(MIKE *stands up and unlocks the door.* BROKEN NOSE *is outside. Looks curiously at* MIKE *and the door.*)
I could have sworn I heard a queer in here.

MIKE: (*Ignoring him*) Done it?

BROKEN NOSE: Not half.

MIKE: So have I.

BROKEN NOSE: I really enjoy tellin' queers t'sod off. There was a lot of them in the French Foreign Legion, y' know. I thought it was goin' t' be all adventure an' killin' people – spent most of me time with me arse t' the wall . . .

MIKE: (*At the other door*) Stay there f' a bit, Bernard, get the suppers ready and –

BROKEN NOSE: Am I like your assistant now? Boss?

MIKE: Er . . . yeah. Assistant manager. But I've got something to do, so . . . A man's got to do what a man's got to do.

BROKEN NOSE: Y' can piss in the sink in the dressin' room if y' want, everyone else does.

(*MIKE goes out.*

As MIKE *goes out, the* COMEDIAN *and his* BOYFRIEND *slam in through the other door. Slam towards the far door.*)

COMEDIAN: Y' don't judge a book by the cover, y' know.

(*They slam out of the room.*)

BROKEN NOSE: I do. I can't read . . . Assistant Manager. (*He grows a couple of inches in height.*)

INT. THE PRIVATE ROOM. NIGHT.

ROSS, FRANK, *the* HEAVIES *and unconscious* MCCARTHUR, *and* MIKE.

FRANK: Y' bluffin'.

MIKE: I'm fuckin' not.

ROSS: Go on then.

MIKE: I've told you – y've got five minutes, at the most t' clean him up, clean the mess up, an' get y'selves out of here.

ROSS: And when the police come.

FRANK: If they're coming.

MIKE I'll just show them around and convince them it was someone's idea of a practical joke.

FRANK: And what if we take you with us as well?

MIKE: Nobody's going anywhere with you – he isn't – and I'm certainly not.

FRANK: Don't believe you.

MIKE: *And no one gets hurt.* Any more.

FRANK: (*Laughing*) I definitely don't believe y', then.

MIKE: Y' will. When the police come. When the letter arrives. And when it gets opened if something happens to me. (*Pause*) Y' see, There Is No Alternative.

ROSS: And what d' you get out of this?

MIKE: I doubt if you'd understand, Mr Ross.

ROSS: Try me.

MIKE: (*Angry*) I know I'm a nobody, but I'm nobody else's nobody!

FRANK: I still say he's bluffin'.

MIKE: *Call it.*

(MIKE *looks at his watch.* ROSS *goes to the door furthest from the foyer. Opens the door. Looks out to the* HEAVIES *outside.*)

ROSS: Get a damp cloth, would you? And a dry one. Now. (*He turns his back into the room. Closes the door over.*) (*Flatly*) Congratulations . . . What do you want doing with him?

MIKE: Well, if he's still got a home to go back to . . .

(ROSS *picks up his overcoat, opens the door again. Motions out.*)

ROSS: Speke Airport.

(FRANK *and the* HEAVY *begin to remove* MCCARTHUR. *One of the* HEAVIES *comes in with the cloths.* ROSS *motions to clean up the blood on the floor.* FRANK *and a* HEAVY *take* MCCARTHUR *out.* ROSS *stands in the doorway, putting his coat on.*)

Every man has a price, Michael. What's yours?

MIKE: You've just paid it.

(ROSS *nods. Goes halfway out of the door. Turns back.*)

ROSS: Oh Frank, you will remind Mr McCarthur about the Official Secrets Act, won't you?

MIKE: I think he already knows.

ROSS: Do you?

MIKE: Off by heart.

ROSS: Don't make a habit of this, mmmm? These are bad times to be a hero . . . Happy New Year.

(ROSS *leaves, as the* HEAVY *wipes up, head down, on his knees.* MIKE *quietly lets his bottle out.*)

INT. THE BODY OF THE CLUB. NIGHT.
As some of the VETERANS *start singing 'Why are we waiting', the* ULSTERMAN *furtively enters the body of the hall.*
CHERYL *is 'supervising' the outgoing food from the kitchen door.*
Points towards a group of tables at the back.
OLD WAITER: What about the Orange Lodge?
> (CHERYL *feels the food with the back of her hand. Looks across.*)
CHERYL: Nah, it's not cold enough yet . . .
> (*The* ULSTERMAN *bends down by* BILLY.)
ULSTERMAN: (*Whispering*) Get me a bottle of whiskey, Billy, I'm going.
BILLY: Now?
ULSTERMAN: Soon. I've made contact, all your troubles are over, now get me the whiskey, I'll need it.
> (*He retreats.* BILLY *looks around. Stands up. Moves towards the bar, feeling into his inside pocket for his wallet.*)

INT. THE FOYER OF THE CLUB. NIGHT.
The ULSTERMAN *comes out of the double doors. He sees* MIKE *at the front doors. Casually. And he sees two police cars come to a hurrying halt outside. And the* ULSTERMAN *goes into a hurrying gallop into the toilets.*

INT. THE BODY OF THE CLUB. NIGHT.
Paddy Burke's table.
BILLY *is leaving the bar, putting a whiskey bottle inside his jacket. Moving towards the foyer.*
TONY BONAPARTE: . . . He's, er, Billy's goin' out, Paddy.
PADDY BURKE: Not now f' Christs sake, I'm havin' me dinner! But if y' want to do somethin', I'll have another pint . . .
> (MRS CAREY *and* WINNIE. MRS CAREY *has pushed her plate away.*)
MRS CAREY: Someone should complain.
WINNIE: The gravy's warm.
> (MRS CAREY *watches the infirm about to be given their dinners. The* VETERANS *increase in voice.*)

MRS CAREY: How can we . . . not with . . . they just
    shouldn't . . .
WINNIE: I know. Still . . . Can I have your meat, Joan?

INT. FOYER OF THE CLUB. NIGHT.
BILLY *in the foyer. Looking towards the foyer doors.*
MIKE *outside, talking to the* POLICEMEN, *and then turning towards
the interior of the club. With the* POLICEMEN.
BILLY *rapidly increases his pace towards the 'Stags' toilets. While
the couple still play on the machines.*
*And we just catch a glimpse of a Mercedes car quietly cruising past
the police cars followed by an ambulance speeding away with all
lights flashing, as* MIKE *leads the policemen in.*

INT. THE 'STAGS' TOILETS. NIGHT.
Inside the far cubicle.
BILLY *standing up. Against the toilet door. The* ULSTERMAN
*standing up. Against the world. As he struggles with something in his
inside jacket pocket.*
ULSTERMAN: You called them, you called them, and y' dead
    Billy, dead –
BILLY: I didn't – and we don't know if –
ULSTERMAN: You an' yours, that fuckin' daughter of yours.
BILLY: Be quiet.
ULSTERMAN: I won't be quiet. Come out, come out!
    (BILLY *realizes what it is.*)
BILLY: You've got a gun.
ULSTERMAN: 'Course I've got a fuckin' gun. I'm a terrorist!
    (BILLY *grabs the* ULSTERMAN *with both hands around the
    neck. Quickly, savagely, quietly, his big hands surrounding the
    scrawny neck. The* ULSTERMAN *chokes. Struggles briefly for
    his gun, then to pull* BILLY *off him. He hasn't got a chance.
    The* ULSTERMAN *goes limp.* BILLY *still goes on. Then lets go
    as suddenly as he started. The* ULSTERMAN *drops on to the
    toilet seat. His head moves absurdly sideways, but he stays on
    the toilet seat.*
    BILLY *stands, hands limply at his sides. Looking. Then reaches
    into the* ULSTERMAN's *inside pocket. Rips the gun out from its
    hiding place.*

He hears heavy steel-tipped footsteps walking down the
toilets towards the cubicles. At least two pairs. A cubicle
door is banged open. BILLY *looks around. No escape. Sits*
down on the ULSTERMAN's *knees. And hears the voices*
from outside.)

MIKE: As y' can see, there's no one gettin' battered in here
either . . .

STEEL TIPS: I know . . . y'd think people'd have better things
to do on New Year's Eve . . .

MIKE: All the lonely people.

OTHER STEEL TIPS: Thank you, Eleanor Rigby.
(*Another door banged.*)

STEEL TIPS: They wouldn't be lonely if I got hold of them.
(*He pushes against the door. Locked.* BILLY *grunts.*)
You busy in there?

BILLY: (*No trace of Ulster*) I'm on overtime.
(*Mild laughter. And they walk away.*

BILLY. *Still sitting on the* ULSTERMAN. *He looks at the gun*
in his hand. Sees his hand is trembling. The body of the
ULSTERMAN *slips sideways, the head bangs against the cubicle*
side wall. BILLY *and the* ULSTERMAN *face on.* BILLY *almost*
looks like a ventriloquist's dummy. Gun on his lap. He checks,
expertly, that it is loaded. Takes a handkerchief out of his
pocket. Wipes the gun.)
. . . Am I going mad in my old age?
(*He sticks the gun in the* ULSTERMAN's *hand. Props him up.*
Stands up. Unlocks the door, peeps out, goes out. Closes the
door behind him. Walks away.)

INT. THE FOYER OF THE CLUB. NIGHT.
The COUPLE *at the machine are winning the jackpot. Loudly. The*
door marked 'Private' is open. Two POLICEMEN *are walking away*
from it. Shrugging their shoulders to the other two POLICEMEN. *The*
four of them walk past MIKE *near the doors.*
BILLY *walks out of the 'Stags' toilets, makes his way behind them as*
MIKE *nods cheerfully at the departing* POLICEMEN. BILLY
approaches the double doors. MIKE *turns away from the exit doors.*
And grins. Huge. But not for long . . .
As BILLY *gets near to the double doors, they open. Six large*

VETERANS *enter the foyer. With coachdriver. And so does the noise of loud very mistaken unpopular music.*

FIRST VET: Fuckin' hell, Billy!

BILLY: . . . What?

SECOND VET: What d' y' mean – 'what'? We can't get our dinner, the band's been let out for the day, they're throwin' wobblers at the next table, an' that bastard Paddy Burke –

BILLY: All right all right –

THIRD VET: It's not all right.

FOURTH VET: And it isn't going to be. (*Pushes the driver*)

DRIVER: All right Grandad, don't take it out on me, y' know.
(*As they march out of the exit doors,* MRS CAREY *goes storming through the double doors at* MIKE. *Who is still watching the* VETS *as they storm out.*)

MRS CAREY: Hey you, you lad! Yes, you! Call y'self a manager!

MIKE: The fancy dress will commen–

MRS CAREY: Frig the fancy dress – they shouldn't be here, mixin' with ordinary people, but if they've got to be here, why do they . . .
(*We see, as her anger diminishes, that she is unable to cope emotionally.*)
. . . I mean, can't you just put them . . . they should be out of sight . . . I DON'T WANT TO BE LIKE THAT!
(*She scuttles tearfully towards the 'Hens' toilets. The jackpot on another machine goes.*)

FRENCH ONION SELLER: . . . *Yis!*
(MIKE *turns away towards the double doors.* BILLY *is ahead of him. He pushes at the doors. Sees* TONY BONAPARTE *behind them. And scuttling already.* BROKEN NOSE *comes rushing out, past* BILLY, *to* MIKE.)

MIKE: Don't, your descriptive powers won't do it justice. (MIKE *goes past* BROKEN NOSE.)

EXT. THE CAR PARK OF THE CLUB. NIGHT.
The coach DRIVER *is surrounded by the* VETS *as he tries to open the passenger door of the coach.*
As he opens it, one of the VETS *wanders down the bus to the back to urinate. As he stands there, in the shadows, he sees a figure running stooped across the gap between buildings, thirty yards away.*

74

*The figure hits a shaft of light. There, clearly, for a second or two, is
a* POLICE MARKSMAN, *rifle in hand.*
The VET *struggles to believe his eyes, splashes his trousers and tries to
walk back towards the others.*
*As we move high above the scene, we hear hoots of disbelief coming
from the* VETS *in the coach.*
A virtual army of POLICEMEN *beginning to arrive and move into
siege-like formation around the area of the club. Transit van after
Transit van begins to appear in the roadways silently surrounding the
club, but not as yet moving forward.*

INT. THE BODY OF THE HALL. NIGHT.
A pandemonium. Of sight and sound.
The INFIRM *are eating their food badly and madly, many are
confused and upset, and this makes them worse. Mouths full, knives
full. Only* JACK *and* MARY, *the couple with some kind of
attachment, seem to be taking things calmly and slowly.*
MATTHEW's *plate slips into his lap. He looks down at it. Looks
anxiously around. Decides to keep it there.* BOBBY *knocks his own*

*plate angrily sideways and off the table. It lands around one of the
very infirm old ladies. She is already half turned around.
She stands up.* MATTHEW *takes his cue from her. He stands up, the
plate sticking to him for a short time, before dropping.
Those still interested amongst the* ORANGE LODGE *party are banging
and demanding either food or the death penalty for teenage
musicians. Some are enjoying the experience.
The vast majority of the audience in the club have little sympathy for
the group. Beer mats begin to fly.
The* CATHOLICS *start to throw the plates first.* PADDY BURKE
throws his at the ORANGE LODGE *tables.
The group loudly approach the end of their first number, a cheerful
ditty entitled 'We're gonna die, die, die'.* MIKE *is already moving
through the club with* BROKEN NOSE *and* CHERYL *towards the
'Stags', trying to avoid missiles and slop.* CHERYL *passes a*
WAITRESS.
Then MACKER *starts cursing the* LEADER, *who is on bass, turns to
the* DRUMMER *to try to get the beat back. Bangs guitars by accident
with the bass guitar of the* LEADER. *Who takes his glasses off.*

Again. And gets walloped instantly over the head by MACKER's
guitar. Not by accident. Hurtles backwards off stage. MACKER *kicks
one of the cymbals up in the air. The cymbal lands on the synthesizer
and knocks it over.* MACKER *tries to kick the drums in. The*
DRUMMER *knocks his way through the drums to get to* MACKER.
BROKEN NOSE: Where's Frank? You'd better get Frank.
>(*And marching from the Foyer, through the hall, come the*
>VETS. *Accordions and strut and 'The Sash'.*
>*While one of the infirm old ladies loses all control. As*
>BOBBY *laughs, she begins hitting him, flat-handed with no
>power. Before* MRS MORGAN *can pull her off,* BOBBY *laughs
>happily.*)
BOBBY: Mother!
>(*The* VETS *march past.*
>*Some of the food intended for the* ORANGE LODGE *gets
>waylaid by some of the* CATHOLICS *as the* WAITRESSES *pass.
>And thrown.*
>*The* VETS *stride through on to the dance area. As the* VETS *who
>have left their drums behind, move towards the stage.*)

FIRST VET: (*At the microphone*) Come on, y' Fenians, where's y' bravery, where's y' balls?

SECOND VET: No balls, no balls, no balls, no balls.

(*Those with the drums join the accordionists on the dance floor. And they are joined by many of the* ORANGE LODGE. *They pound through 'The Sash'. Victorious and dancing.*

MIKE, CHERYL *and* BROKEN NOSE *look on.*

A pint glass smashes near the first VET. *He moves away from the microphone. We catch a glimpse of* TONY BONAPARTE *about to throw another.*)

CHERYL: We'll see who's got no balls . . .

(*She moves away from* MIKE *and* BROKEN NOSE.

MIKE *sees* CHERYL *reinforcing the* CATHOLICS *in their fancy dress, moving to either side of the* VETS *and the accordions and the drums. Towards the stage.*

PADDY BURKE *and* TONY BONAPARTE *have stayed where they were, although* PADDY BURKE *occasionally, mindlessly, throws something.* TONY BONAPARTE *is watching* BILLY.

BILLY, *still, almost alone, in his place, slumped back, hardly*

78

watching, seemingly disinterested. MR *and* MRS O'GORMAN
have stayed too, still holding hands.
The INFIRM *howl and mumble on.* MRS MORGAN *defeated.*
MR O'GORMAN *turns slightly to* BILLY. *Talks quietly.*)
MR O'GORMAN: . . . No wonder you were crazy as a kid, Billy
. . . y' must have known it'd all come to this . . .
(BILLY *shakes his head. Expressionless.* MR O'GORMAN
*struggles to stand up. Gives up for a time as his wife pulls at his
hand and looks up at him. Not far short of tears.*
Then out of the vibrant violent 'The Sash' we begin to hear
CHERYL's *voice at the microphone. Gaining confidence,*
strength and voice.
As she begins to sing 'Ave Maria'.
We see her on stage. Joined by many CATHOLICS. *Facing the*
ORANGE LODGE. *Voices ringing out. 'The Sash' and 'Ave*
Maria' flood the room.
We return to MR O'GORMAN, MRS O'GORMAN *and* BILLY.)

(*Loudly*) I've got to go and pay a penny, Freda.

MRS O'GORMAN: (*Nodding and quietly*) Don't be too long.
Please.

(*As* MR O'GORMAN *stands, so does* BILLY.)

MR O'GORMAN: Are you going?

BILLY: I've gone.

(*He walks towards the exit, past the* INFIRM. *And near the*
CATHOLIC *table.*

TONY BONAPARTE *and* PADDY BURKE *rise.* TONY *grabs an
empty pint glass as he leads* PADDY *away. After* BILLY. MR
O'GORMAN *is already limping behind them.*

We return briefly to BROKEN NOSE *and* MIKE. BROKEN
NOSE *has never seen so many broken rules. He has hold of*
MIKE's *sleeve by the elbow.*)

BROKEN NOSE: Y've got to do something.

MIKE: *Now?* When they're having such a good time? Don't be a
spoilsport . . . And she can really sing, Cheryl, can't she?

INT. THE FOYER. NIGHT.

BILLY *walks through the double doors into the foyer. He approaches
the exit doors. Heavy-footed. Knackered.* LITTLE BO-PEEP *and*
FRENCH ONION SELLER *play on.*

TONY BONAPARTE *has already opened the double doors.* PADDY
BURKE *peering behind him, as they advance.*

TONY BONAPARTE *hustles up behind* BILLY, *pint glass in hand.
This is the only violence he has ever been capable of, and only just,
at that.*

As he nears upon BILLY *nervously,* MR O'GORMAN *walks through
the double doors.* PADDY *is a few yards away from him.* TONY
BONAPARTE *has the glass raised.* MR O'GORMAN *sees what is
about to happen. But too late.*

TONY BONAPARTE *crashes the pint glass across the back of* BILLY's
head a split second after MR O'GORMAN *has shouted.*

MR O'GORMAN: Billy!

(BILLY *is knocked against the nearest wall,* TONY BONAPARTE
*hits him again, and then grabs and throws him towards
the* 'Stags' *toilets nearby. As* BILLY *turns to protect himself,*
TONY *catches him another glancing blow across the head.
As he does this, and* PADDY BURKE *sticks towards the noise,*

MRS CAREY *comes out of the 'Hens' toilets, eyes black and reddened, and sees the tail end of it all.*
She sees TONY BONAPARTE *banging* BILLY *into the 'Stags' and disappearing, while* PADDY *and* MR O'GORMAN *make their own way towards the toilet.*
She hurries through the double doors.)

INT. THE 'STAGS' TOILET. NIGHT.
BILLY *is on the floor. Groaning and breathing heavily.* TONY BONAPARTE *above him, but not capable of a fully frontal attack.* TWO MEN *have just finished at the urinal. Recoil from it all especially when* PADDY BURKE *enters.*
TONY BONAPARTE: (*To the men*) Beat it, beat it!
    (*The* MEN *struggle away.* PADDY BURKE *lashes out lunatically with his stick as he sees their vague shadows passing him. Approaches the noise of* BILLY.
    TONY BONAPARTE *goes to the light switch.*
    MR O'GORMAN *enters the toilets.*

BIRKBECK LIBRARY COLLEGE

MR O'GORMAN *realizes what is going on. Raises his stick.*
TONY BONAPARTE *hits the light switch.*
Just as MR O'GORMAN *hits* TONY BONAPARTE.
Darkness.
The light comes back on.
TONY BONAPARTE *holds his cheekbone and the light switch,*
looking shocked and in a nearby mirror.
MR O'GORMAN *holding his stick and looking at it in equal*
shock. To hit someone once in your life is enough. And he opens
the door and departs rapidly on his sticks.
PADDY BURKE, *stick cracking against the tiled floor, is hitting*
out at BILLY. BILLY *is scampering and grunting.*)

INT. THE MAIN BODY OF THE CLUB. NIGHT.
The celebrations and songs continue. MRS CAREY *is informing the*
CATHOLIC *element.* MR O'GORMAN *limps through the* ORANGE
LODGE. CATHOLICS *move off the stage in the middle of* CHERYL's
encore of 'Ave Maria' and the ORANGE LODGE's 'The Sash'.
They all begin to move out towards the foyer. CATHOLICS *first.*
Shoving and knocking and barging each other, pulling wigs.
It is 1931 all over again.
The INFIRM *continue, but slowly coming down.* MRS MORGAN *and*
the WARDEN *working wildly overtime.*
MIKE *and* BROKEN NOSE *see the exodus.*
MIKE: I er . . . didn't you tell me that the foyer was your
    responsibility, Bernard? . . . At some point tonight. (*He*
    moves away towards the stage and CHERYL. *Turns back and*
    motions with his eyes towards the foyer doors.)
BROKEN NOSE: . . . All this for two pounds eighty-six an hour
    . . . (*He moves away.*)
    (MIKE *jumps on to the stage, approaches* CHERYL. *Stands with*
    her. He surveys the audience. Those who aren't wild and
    motivated still number around three hundred, even though they
    are perplexed, distant and distraught.
    He looks at CHERYL. *Takes hold of the microphone. Sings.*)
MIKE: 'If you need me, I want you to call me . . .'
    (*She joins him.*)

INT. FOYER OF THE CLUB. NIGHT.
Men and women cascading into the foyer.
Bright and alive and dangerous and difficult.
All trying to get into the 'Stags' toilets.
The CATHOLICS *have a slight head start.* MRS CAREY *was quicker.*

INT. THE 'STAGS' TOILETS. NIGHT.
Crowded.
Lit and then unlit.
It stays unlit more often. The CATHOLICS *have the advantage of*
numbers for some time.
People are remembering all their spent passions.
Men and women struggle for the light switch and against each other.
We hear cries of faith, revenge, time and specifics. We also hear some
cries of pain.
But we focus on the fight between BILLY *and* PADDY BURKE.
A raging mad bull of a fight.

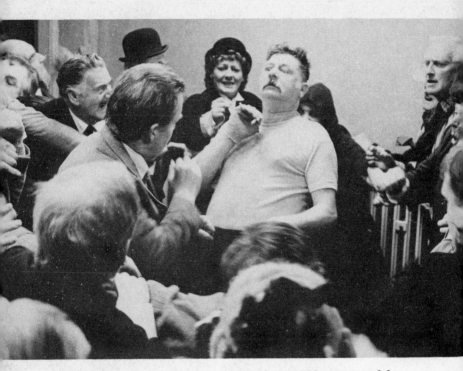

Two men, one barely able to see, the other in darkness most of the time. From wall to wall and cubicle to cubicle.

With stick and fist and elbows and head, knees and groin.

Doors crash, windows smash.

At one point a toilet is flushed.

BILLY and PADDY BURKE are young men again. In mind and mood anyway.

The light comes on for longer than before.

We see BROKEN NOSE trying to gain entry.

BROKEN NOSE: Return to the hall now, please.

> (He is mobbed away and out. Hurtling through the toilet doorway into the foyer.
>
> Before the lights go out, we see the PRIEST land a right hook, and we see OLIVER HARDY, supported by one hand on the cistern and one arm around his wife, kicking a VET in the goolies.

BILLY and PADDY BURKE move unsteadily down the toilets

towards the end cubicle. One has his sword, the other his sight.
BILLY *has his passion back,* PADDY *has never lost his.*
They catch the light from outside. PADDY *whirls his stick.*
BILLY *can see it this time. Catches it whipping in mid-stroke,*
holds on despite the pain. Tears it away from PADDY'*s grip.*
Hits PADDY *with it once. Then throws it away.*
BILLY *crashes* PADDY *against the far wall, by the end cubicle.*
Then BILLY *finishes him like a boxer.*
A blow to the midriff, bending PADDY *down, then an uppercut*
to the jaw, bringing him up. A right cross and then a left.
Sinking him down, on to his knees, falling against BILLY. *And*
holding on.
BILLY *grabs him as he starts to fall again. Lifts* PADDY *up.*
Bangs PADDY'*s head again and again against the far wall.*
The lights go on and off. Once.
A beer glass smashes near BILLY *and* PADDY. BILLY *continues*

to beat PADDY. *Wild brief seconds.*
BILLY *holds* PADDY *against the far toilet cubicle, hurls him in.*
We see the dead ULSTERMAN *slumped grotesquely against the*
cubicle wall, open-mouthed and ashen. Gun in hand.
BILLY *throws* PADDY *against and across the* ULSTERMAN.
They collide like two lovers around each other.
BILLY *leans against the closed toilet door.*
There is a brief silence. In the 'Stags'. Only the noise from
outside. Then there is a wild cheer from the ORANGE LODGE
Some begin to approach BILLY.)

INT. THE FOYER OF THE CLUB. NIGHT.
A defeated and dishevelled BROKEN NOSE *leans against the public*
telephone.
Many people try to crowd into the 'Stags'.
LITTLE BO-PEEP *still tries the machines.*
THE FRENCH ONION SELLER *counts his money.*
BROKEN NOSE *gets through on the phone.*
BROKEN NOSE: . . . Police . . . yeah, Charleston Club, Stanley
    Road . . . a . . . like disturbance . . . friggin' hundreds, girl
    . . . as soon as y' can . . .
    (BROKEN NOSE *goes to put the phone down.*
    And crashing through and knocking down the double doors of
    the foyer come the combined forces of half of Liverpool's police
    force. With guns and postures.
    We just catch a taste of BROKEN NOSE *holding and looking at*
    the phone. Then looking at the police. Disbelieving.)

INT. THE 'STAGS' TOILET. NIGHT.
As the POLICE *burst in, and try to race down the toilet.*
Blocked by everyone, accidentally or otherwise, trapped in the small
space.
Some of the VETS *hurry towards* BILLY. QUASIMODO *and*
DONALD DUCK *go in search of* PADDY BURKE.
The POLICE *are screaming and threatening; both* ORANGE LODGE
and CATHOLICS *come together in sullen awkwardness.*
The VETS *have enough time to pull* BILLY *into their midst and move*
towards the middle of the cubicles.
QUASIMODO *and* DONALD DUCK *see* PADDY BURKE *draped*

across the ULSTERMAN *and the gun. And the toilet.*
They just stare. Till they are virtually lifted and thrown away by the
POLICE. *Who then stop in their tracks themselves. At the cubicle*
door.
A SENIOR POLICEMAN *struggles through the mob.*
SENIOR POLICEMAN: All right, all right, what's goin' on in
  here?
QUASIMODO: We've all got diarrhoea . . .
  (*Laughter from all, as they begin to get ordered out. And the*
  POLICE *surround the end cubicle.*)

INT. THE STAGE, THE CHARLESTON CLUB. NIGHT.
The Fancy Dress competition.
The CATHOLICS *in a thin line across the stage, slightly set back from*
the front. Facing out. Some with cuts and bruises.
The FRENCH ONION SELLER *and* LITTLE BO-PEEP *breathlessly*
arriving and joining the end of the line. All three CHARLIE
CHAPLINS *endlessly bend their legs and draw circles with their*
sticks. QUASIMODO *is humped up next to* STAN LAUREL *and*

OLIVER HARDY. QUASIMODO *is talking tight-lipped to* OLIVER HARDY.

Walking along the line is CHERYL *in the sequinned dress, with a very self-important* BROKEN NOSE.

QUASIMODO: . . . So what he reckon happened is that the dead feller, the Irishman, must have had his gun trained on Paddy while he was fightin' ready to kill him like, an' even though, even though Paddy was in the state he was in, when Paddy went through the doorway, he still had enough strength –

(CHERYL *and* BROKEN NOSE *approach.* QUASIMODO *contorts his face.*)

'The bells, the bells!'

(CHERYL *and* BROKEN NOSE *move down the line, past* LAUREL *and* HARDY. STAN LAUREL *scratches her head.*)

– he still had enough strength, when he saw the gun, to throw himself at the Irishman an' strangle him! Before he collapsed himself.

OLIVER HARDY: He's a fuckin' hero, isn't he, mad though he is. Has Paddy said anythin' about it?

(CHERYL *and* BROKEN NOSE *return.*)

QUASIMODO: 'The bells, the bells!' . . . Nah, he was unconscious when the ambulance took him away. Tony Stavoni went with him.

OLIVER HARDY: To look after him, like?

QUASIMODO: No, he was unconscious as well, Billy the Beast hit him on the way out the toilets . . .

(BILLY *the Beast's table. More drinks than the table has room for surround him. So do his wellwishers and backslappers. He takes it all, expressionless, as* VETS *sing 'Paddy was a bastard' around him.*

The INFIRM *are no longer at their table.*

As MIKE *announces the winners of the Fancy Dress, from the front of the stage, flanked by* CHERYL *and* BROKEN NOSE, *we glimpse some of the sly looks of jealousy and disappointment from the losers, particularly* MRS CAREY. *And the placid joy of the winners.*)

MIKE: Ladies and gentlemen, first prize in our Fancy Dress Competition tonight goes to . . . Laurel and Hardy!

(*Absolutely no applause.*)

EXT. OUTSIDE THE CHARLESTON CLUB. MIDNIGHT.
Churchbells chime midnight.
MIKE *is kissing* CHERYL. BROKEN NOSE *waiting his turn
carefully, combing his quiff. He tries to step in for his kiss twice, but
each time* CHERYL *and* MIKE *go back for more.*
The CATHOLIC *section celebrating together.*
The ORANGE LODGE *element together.*
Both sets singing, separately, 'Should auld acquaintance . . .'
*As they break the circles and begin to hug each other, a figure slips
away from the* ORANGE LODGE *group, quietly going through the
crowds, turning a corner and walking away.*
It is BILLY.
*A taxi approaches. He puts his hand up for it. It is occupied. He
keeps walking. Slowly.*

INT. THE BODY OF THE HALL. NIGHT.
Empty.
Save for BROKEN NOSE, MIKE *and* CHERYL. *At a table by the
bar, eating toast and drinking tea or coffee.* BROKEN NOSE *has his
overcoat on.* MIKE *and* CHERYL *are dressed as we first saw them.*
BROKEN NOSE *stands.*
MIKE: Home?
BROKEN NOSE: It's either that or an orgy, I'm not certain . . .
MIKE: I know, same with me.
CHERYL: An' me.
MIKE: Well, when y' get home, give her one for me.
BROKEN NOSE: I don't know if me mother'd appreciate that.
    (*He goes off through the club and out.*)
MIKE: He lives with his mother?
CHERYL: Yeah . . . I don't. Live with my mother. Or his.
    I don't live with anyone. Any more.
MIKE: (*Standing up*) I do.
CHERYL: (*Joining him*) So it's my place . . .
MIKE: . . . I'm a happily married man.
CHERYL: Yeah. Well, it won't last. It never does.
    (*She begins to walk out. He watches her go.*)
MIKE: Cheryl.
    (*She stops.*)

89

EXT. TWELFTH OF JULY CLUB. NIGHT.
Very still, the Union Jack hanging limp in the cold air. BILLY
walks into the club.

INT. TWELFTH OF JULY CLUB MAIN HALL. NIGHT.
The hall is dimly lit. Barely seen Orange Order paraphernalia.
BILLY *walks through.*

INT. TWELFTH OF JULY CLUB. NIGHT.
BILLY *walks into small side room. The splashes of orange previously
seen now seem dark and colourless. The framed pillowslip –
embroidered by the loyalist internees, cage eleven, the Maze prison
camp – is almost in black and white.* BILLY *sits down in a chair by
the telephone, slumps. Picks up the telephone. Dials. Waits.*
BILLY: Elizabeth, it's me . . . and you. Happy New Year.
　　Listen, girl, I want to speak to Brendan. *Brendan. (Lightly)*
　　My son-in-law . . . Brendan, would you . . . would you
　　consider it sentimental of me after all these years, if I was to
　　wish you a Happy New Year?
　　*(The credits come up on him as he quietly, flatly, continues the
　　rest of the conversation.)*